Dr. Jekyll and Mr. Hyde

ROBERT LOUIS STEVENSON

SADDLEBACK
EDUCATIONAL PUBLISHING

Saddleback's *Illustrated Classics*™

SADDLEBACK
EDUCATIONAL PUBLISHING

Three Watson
Irvine, CA 92618-2767
Website: www.sdlback.com

ISBN-13: 978-1-56254-894-0
ISBN-10: 1-56254-894-8
eBook: 978-1-60291-146-8

Printed in China

Welcome to
Saddleback's *Illustrated Classics*™

We are proud to welcome you to Saddleback's *Illustrated Classics*™. Saddleback's *Illustrated Classics*™ was designed specifically for the classroom to introduce readers to many of the great classics in literature. Each text, written and adapted by teachers and researchers, has been edited using the Dale-Chall vocabulary system. In addition, much time and effort has been spent to ensure that these high-interest stories retain all of the excitement, intrigue, and adventure of the original books.

With these graphically *Illustrated Classics*™, you learn what happens in the story in a number of different ways. One way is by reading the words a character says. Another way is by looking at the drawings of the character. The artist can tell you what kind of person a character is and what he or she is thinking or feeling.

This series will help you to develop confidence and a sense of accomplishment as you finish each novel. The stories in Saddleback's *Illustrated Classics*™ are fun to read. And remember, fun motivates!

Overview

Everyone deserves to read the best literature our language has to offer. Saddleback's *Illustrated Classics*™ was designed to acquaint readers with the most famous stories from the world's greatest authors, while teaching essential skills. You will learn how to:

- Establish a purpose for reading
- Use prior knowledge
- Evaluate your reading
- Listen to the language as it is written
- Extend literary and language appreciation through discussion and writing activities

Reading is one of the most important skills you will ever learn. It provides the key to all kinds of information. By reading the *Illustrated Classics*™, you will develop confidence and the self-satisfaction that comes from accomplishment—a solid foundation for any reader.

Step-By-Step

The following is a simple guide to using and enjoying each of your *Illustrated Classics*™. To maximize your use of the learning activities provided, we suggest that you follow these steps:

1. *Listen!* We suggest that you listen to the read-along. (At this time, please ignore the beeps.) You will enjoy this wonderfully dramatized presentation.

2. *Pre-reading Activities.* After listening to the audio presentation, the pre-reading activities in the Activity Book prepare you for reading the story by setting the scene, introducing more difficult vocabulary words, and providing some short exercises.

3. *Reading Activities.* Now turn to the "While you are reading" portion of the Activity Book, which directs you to make a list of story-related facts. Read-along while listening to the audio presentation. (This time pay attention to the beeps, as they indicate when each page should be turned.)

4. *Post-reading Activities.* You have successfully read the story and listened to the audio presentation. Now answer the multiple-choice questions and other activities in the Activity Book.

Remember,

"Today's readers are tomorrow's leaders."

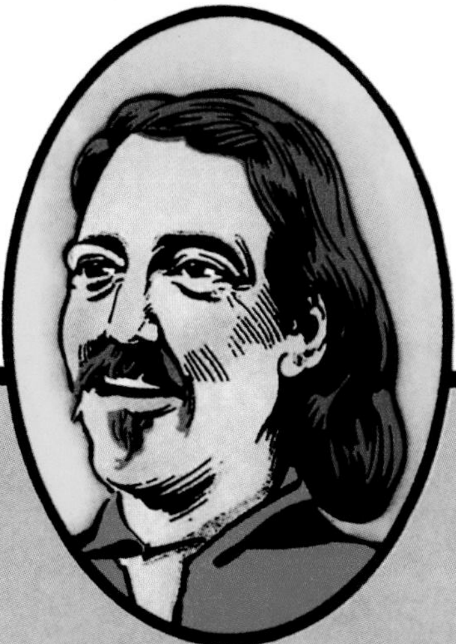

Robert Louis Stevenson

Robert Louis Balfour Stevenson, who came to be known as Louis to avoid confusion with an older cousin, was born in Edinburgh, Scotland, in 1850. An industrious person, he carried two books with him always—one to read and one in which to write.

Stevenson's interest in human psychology and fascination with the conflict of good and evil in man prompted him to write *The Strange Case of Dr. Jekyll and Mr. Hyde* in 1886. Partially because of his Calvinist upbringing, he thought that man was always suppressing his evil nature. This nature, so long held back, breaks loose violently in the character of Edward Hyde.

Stevenson, a collector of ideas, often borrowed from other writers, but his own style was unmistakable. *Treasure Island*, Stevenson's first successful book, was written in 1881. In 1885, while hard at work on *Kidnapped, A Child's Garden of Verses* was published. In 1887, he began *The Master of Ballantrae*, finishing it in 1889. Stevenson died in 1894, never completing his final book, *Weir of Hermiston*, referred to by many critics as his finest work.

Although plagued by illness throughout his life, Stevenson was a restless adventurer. He traveled extensively, married an American and retreated for health reasons to the South Sea Islands in 1889. Here, he established himself as the "tusitala" or the "teller of tales" to the natives.

Saddleback's *Illustrated Classics*™

Dr. Jekyll and Mr. Hyde

ROBERT LOUIS STEVENSON

THE MAIN CHARACTERS

UTTERSON

DR. JEKYLL

DR. LANYON

POOLE

MR. HYDE

LANDLADY

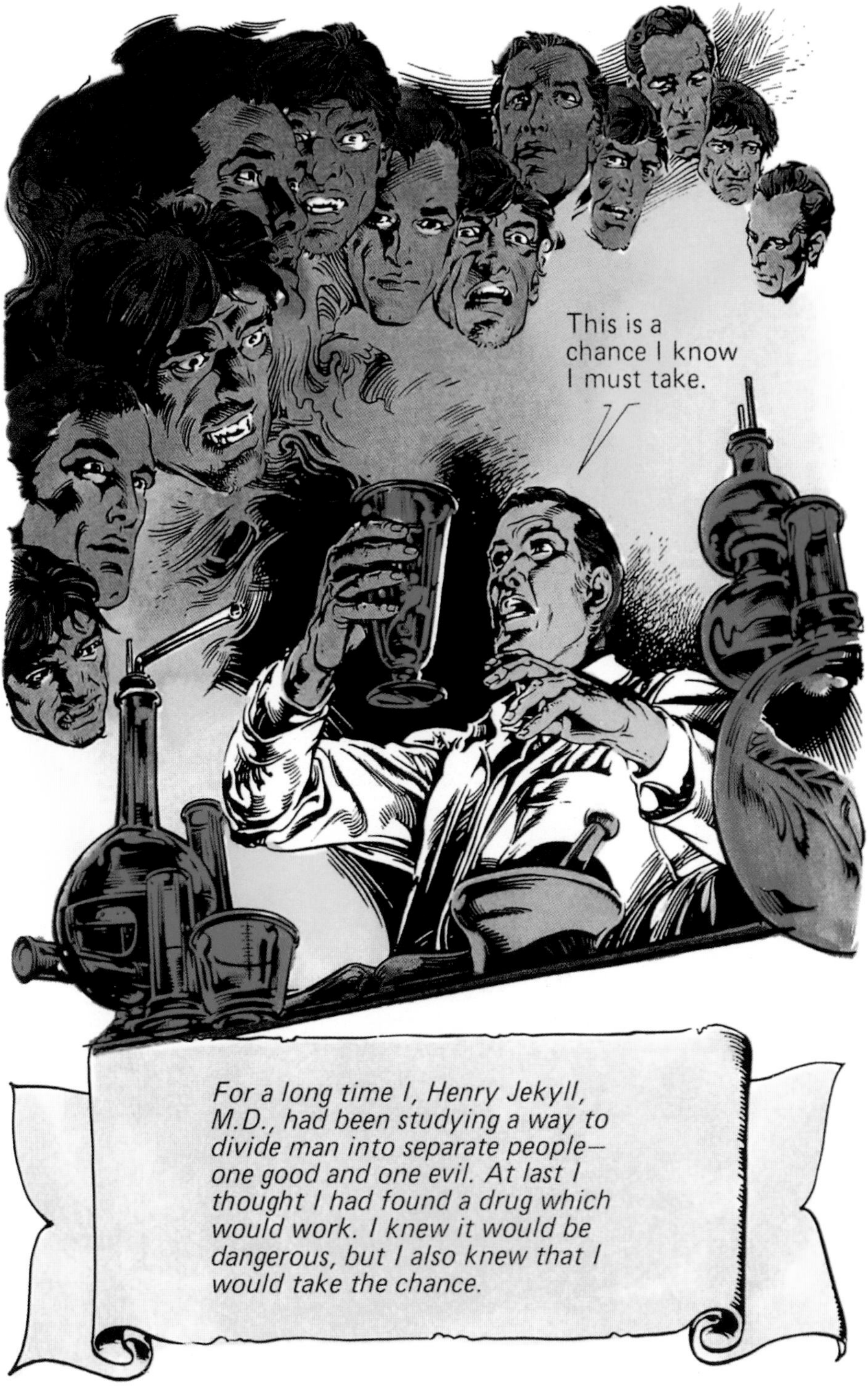
This is a chance I know I must take.
For a long time I, Henry Jekyll, M.D., had been studying a way to divide man into separate people—one good and one evil. At last I thought I had found a drug which would work. I knew it would be dangerous, but I also knew that I would take the chance.

I was born into a wealthy family. I became a well-known doctor.

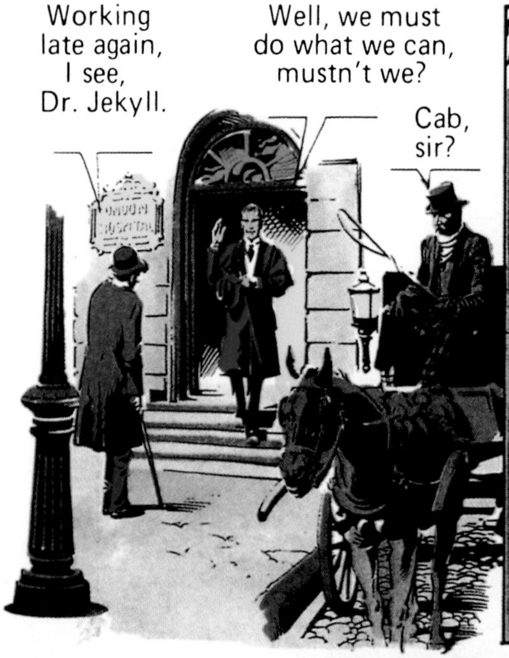
Working
late again,
I see,
Dr. Jekyll.
Well, we must
do what we can,
mustn't we?
Cab,
sir?

As Dr. Jekyll, I was leading two lives. My evil life, however, was kept hidden.

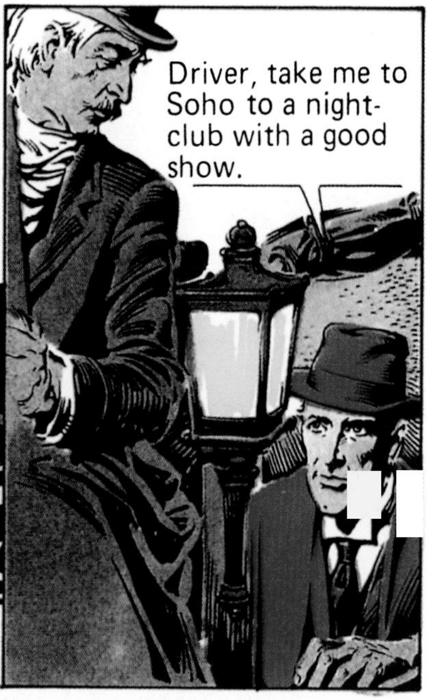
Driver, take me to
Soho to a night-
club with a good
show.

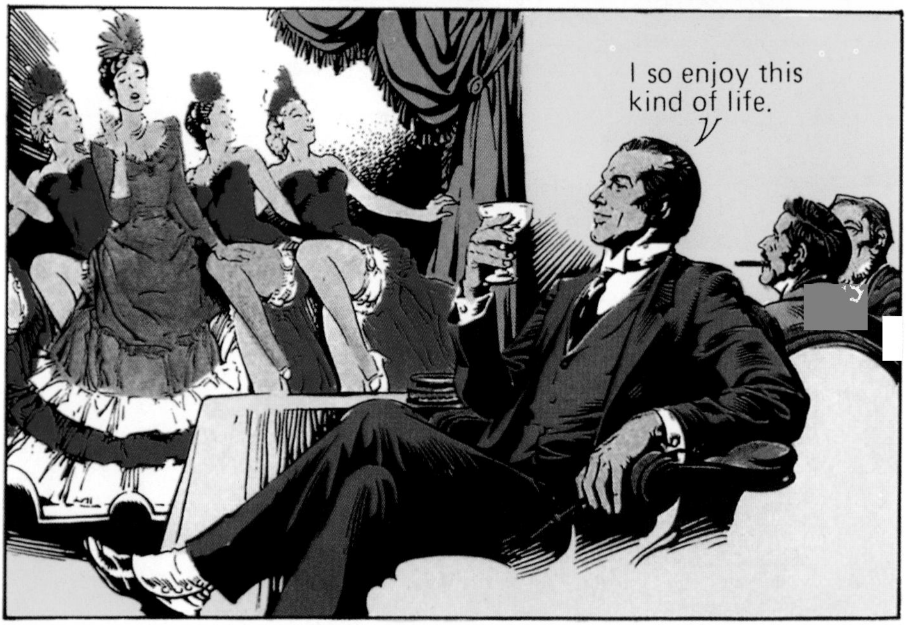
I so enjoy this
kind of life.

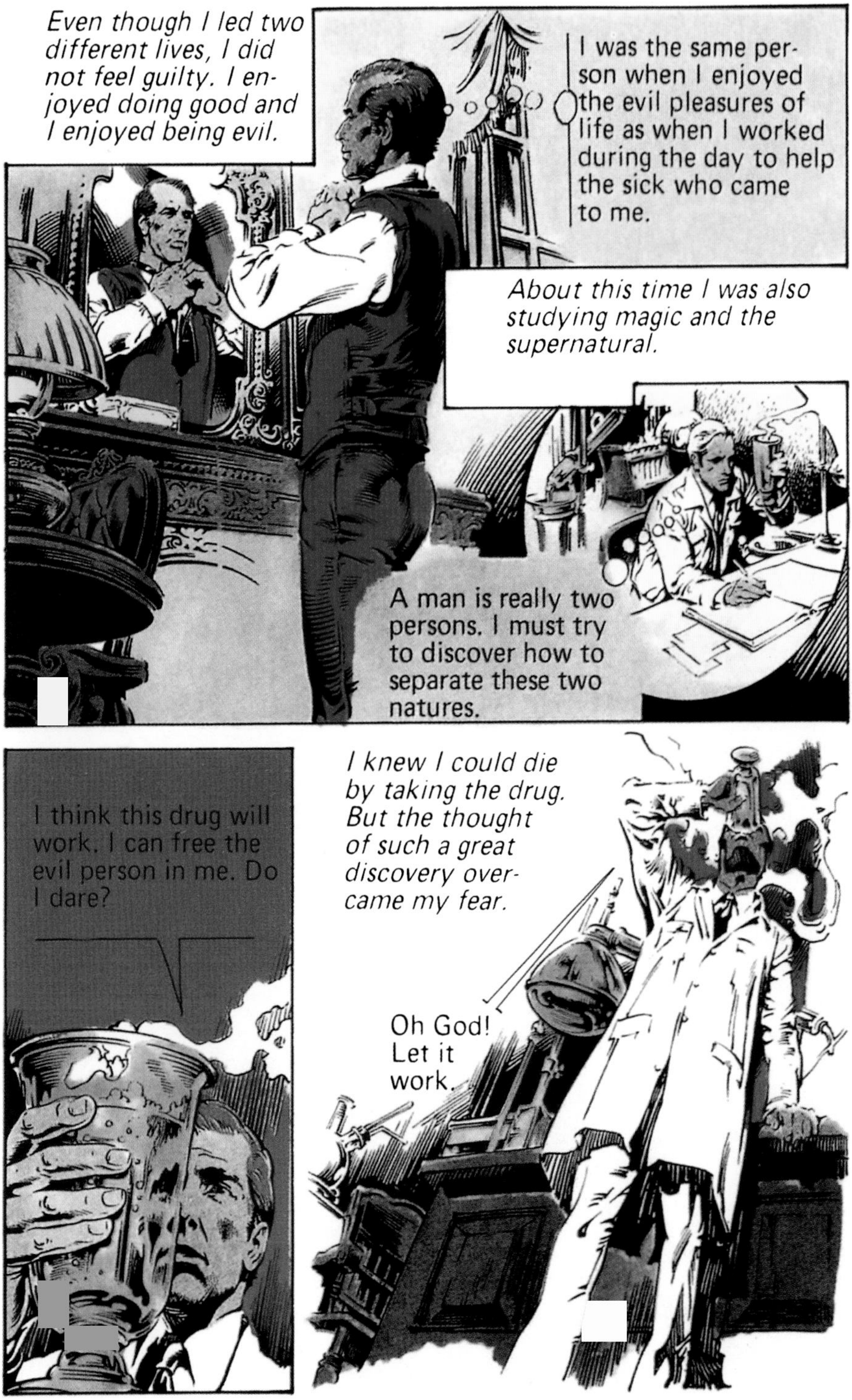
Even though I led two different lives, I did not feel guilty. I enjoyed doing good and I enjoyed being evil.
I was the same person when I enjoyed the evil pleasures of life as when I worked during the day to help the sick who came to me.
About this time I was also studying magic and the supernatural.
A man is really two persons. I must try to discover how to separate these two natures.
I think this drug will work. I can free the evil person in me. Do I dare?
I knew I could die by taking the drug. But the thought of such a great discovery overcame my fear.
Oh God! Let it work.

The most terrible pain followed.

My bones ached.

I thought I would die.

When the pain stopped, I felt weak, as if I had been ill for a long time.

Right away I knew this person I had changed into was ugly and evil. But I was glad.

As I was enjoying these new feelings, I suddenly noticed that my appearance had changed.

Welcome, you are Edward Hyde, the evil side of my nature.

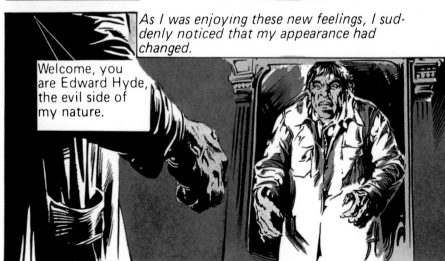

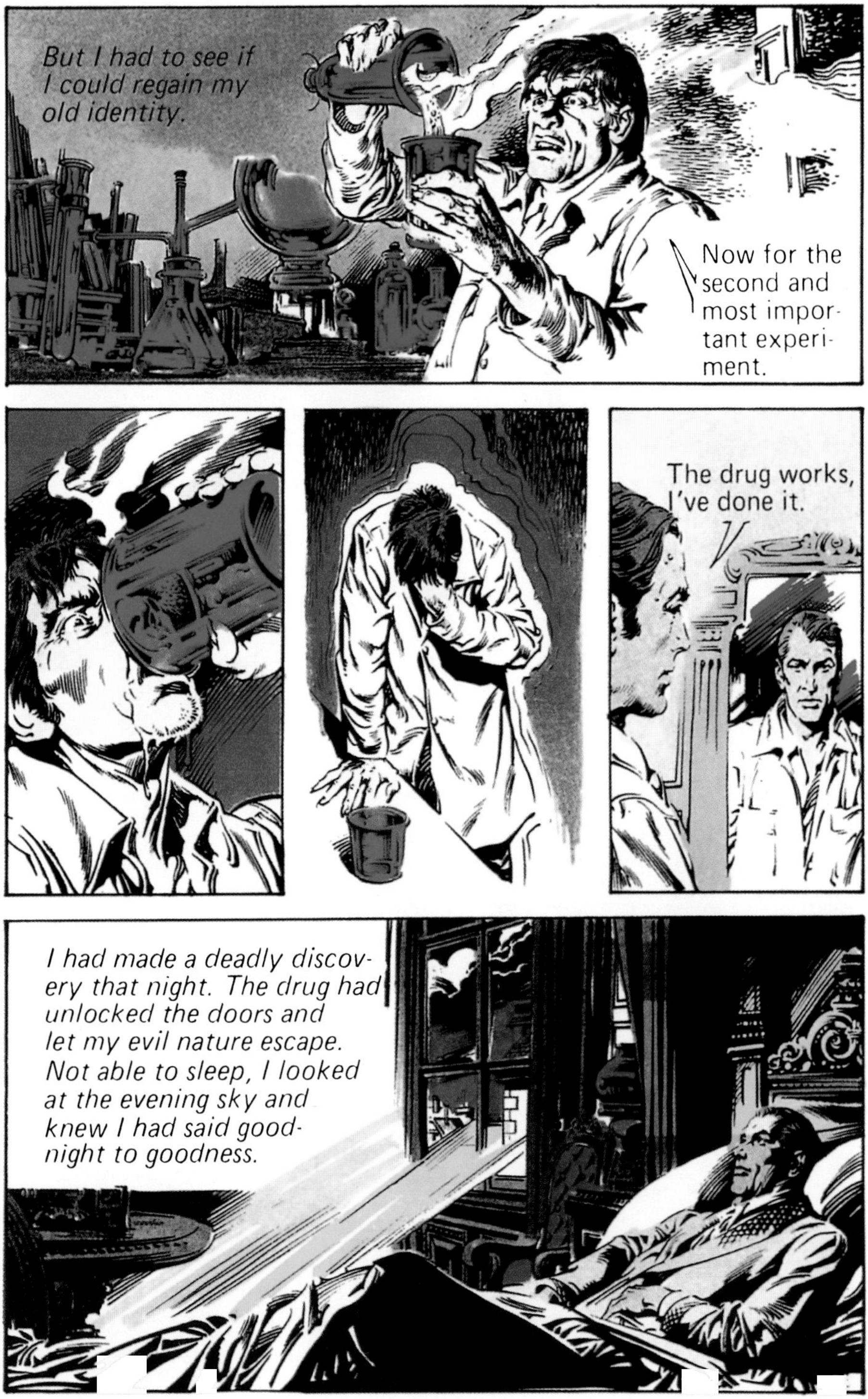
But I had to see if I could regain my old identity.
Now for the second and most important experiment.
The drug works, I've done it.
I had made a deadly discovery that night. The drug had unlocked the doors and let my evil nature escape. Not able to sleep, I looked at the evening sky and knew I had said goodnight to goodness.

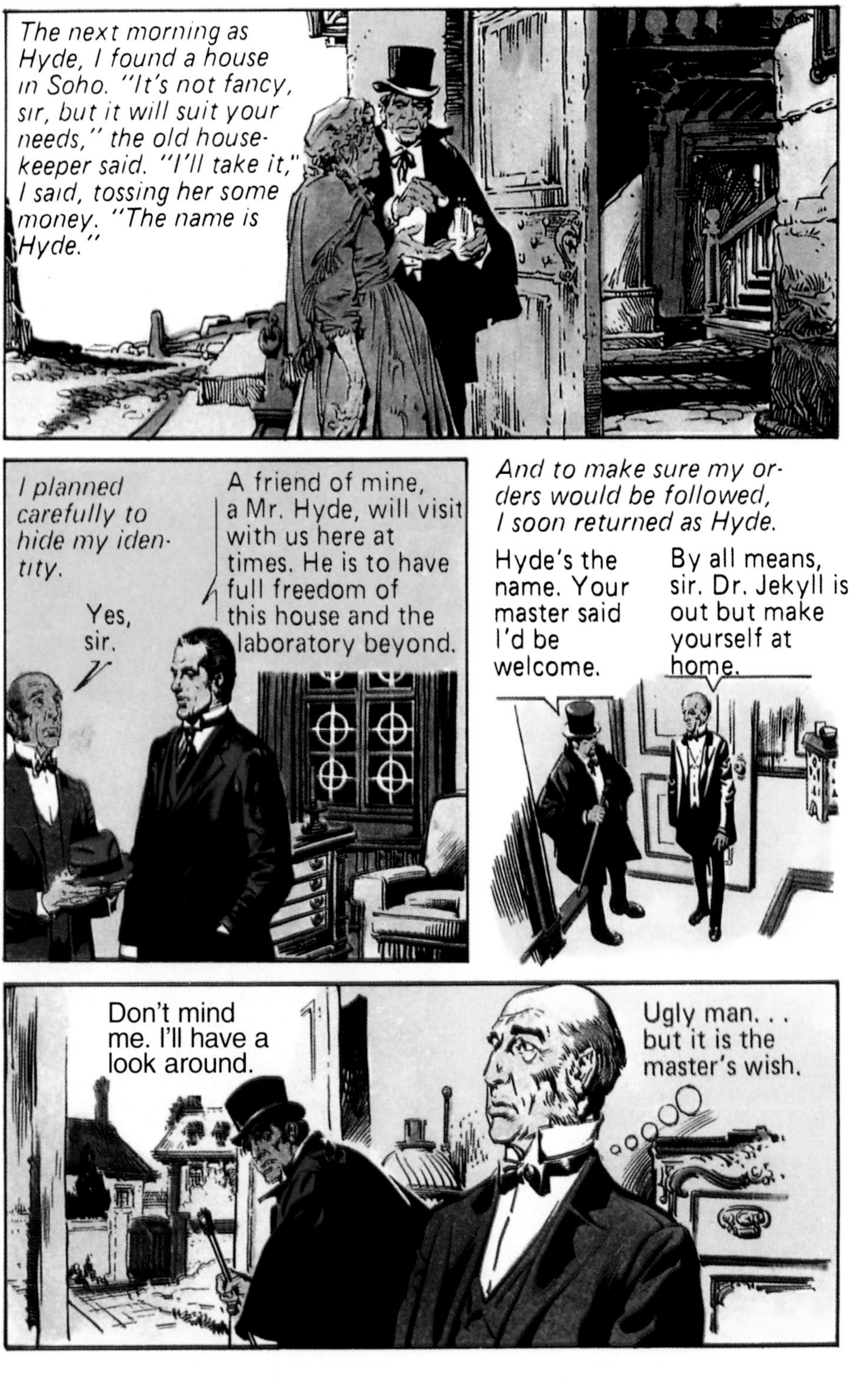
The next morning as Hyde, I found a house in Soho. "It's not fancy, sir, but it will suit your needs," the old housekeeper said. "I'll take it," I said, tossing her some money. "The name is Hyde."
I planned carefully to hide my identity.
A friend of mine, a Mr. Hyde, will visit with us here at times. He is to have full freedom of this house and the laboratory beyond.
Yes, sir.
And to make sure my orders would be followed, I soon returned as Hyde.
Hyde's the name. Your master said I'd be welcome.
By all means, sir. Dr. Jekyll is out but make yourself at home.
Don't mind me. I'll have a look around.
Ugly man. . . but it is the master's wish.

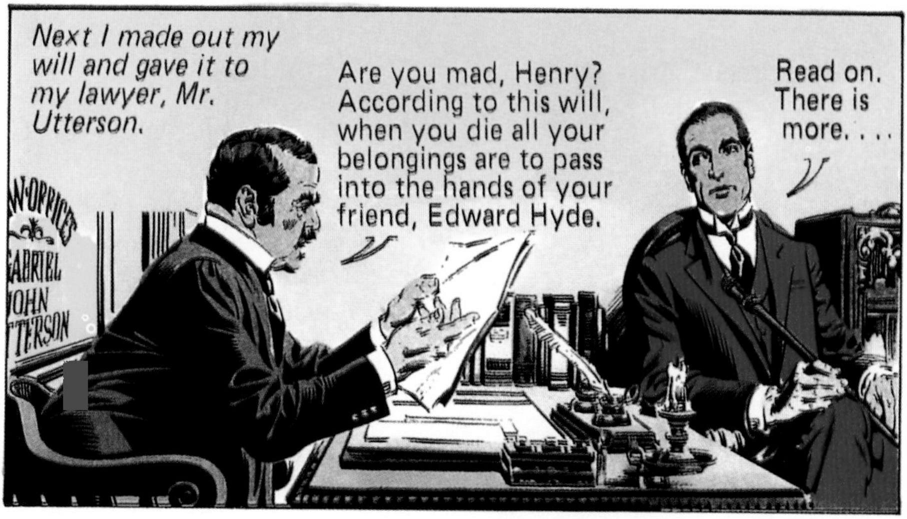
Next I made out my will and gave it to my lawyer, Mr. Utterson.
Are you mad, Henry? According to this will, when you die all your belongings are to pass into the hands of your friend, Edward Hyde.
Read on. There is more. . . .
LAW OFFICES
GABRIEL JOHN UTTERSON

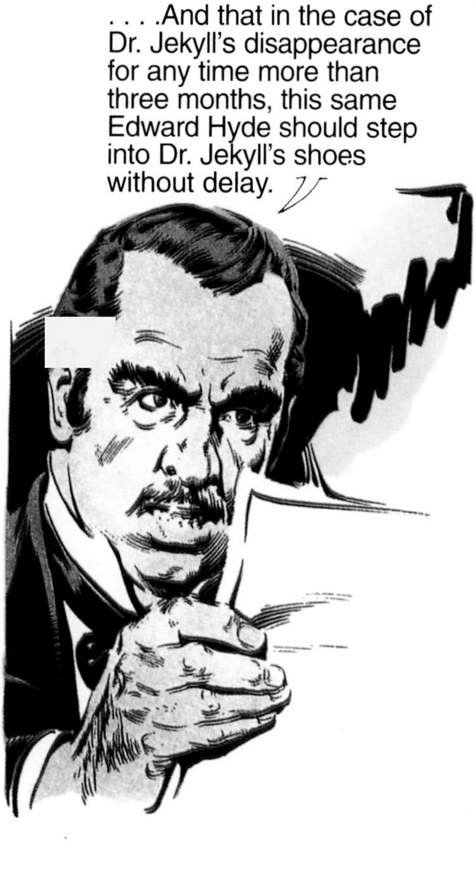
. . . .And that in the case of Dr. Jekyll's disappearance for any time more than three months, this same Edward Hyde should step into Dr. Jekyll's shoes without delay.

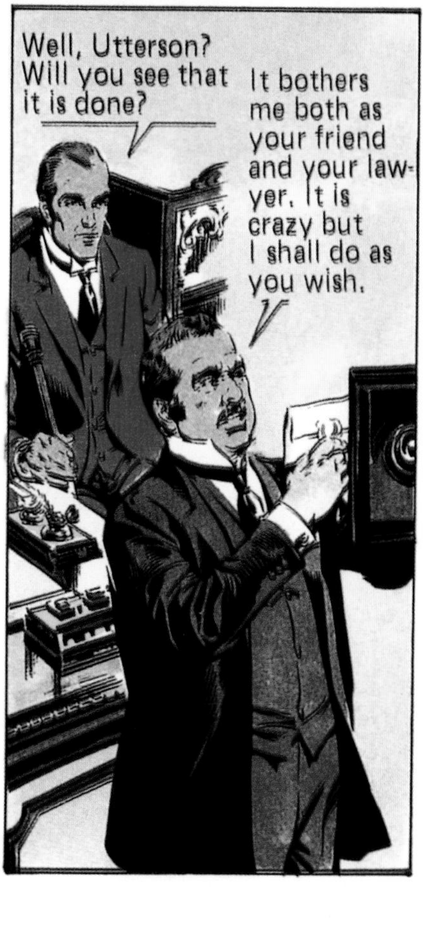
Well, Utterson? Will you see that it is done?
It bothers me both as your friend and your lawyer. It is crazy but I shall do as you wish.

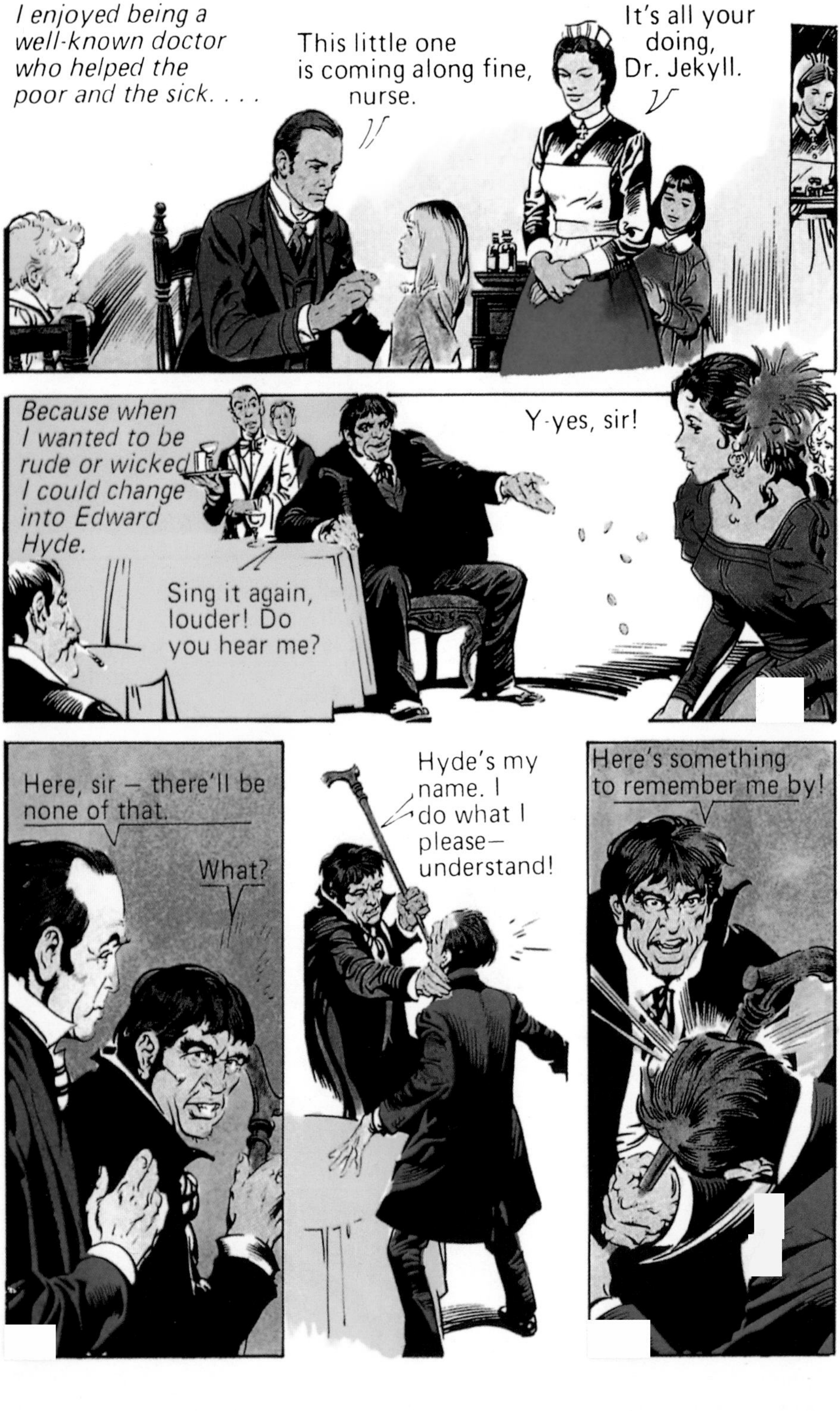
I enjoyed being a well-known doctor who helped the poor and the sick. . . .
This little one is coming along fine, nurse.
It's all your doing, Dr. Jekyll.
Because when I wanted to be rude or wicked I could change into Edward Hyde.
Sing it again, louder! Do you hear me?
Y-yes, sir!
Here, sir — there'll be none of that.
What?
Hyde's my name. I do what I please— understand!
Here's something to remember me by!

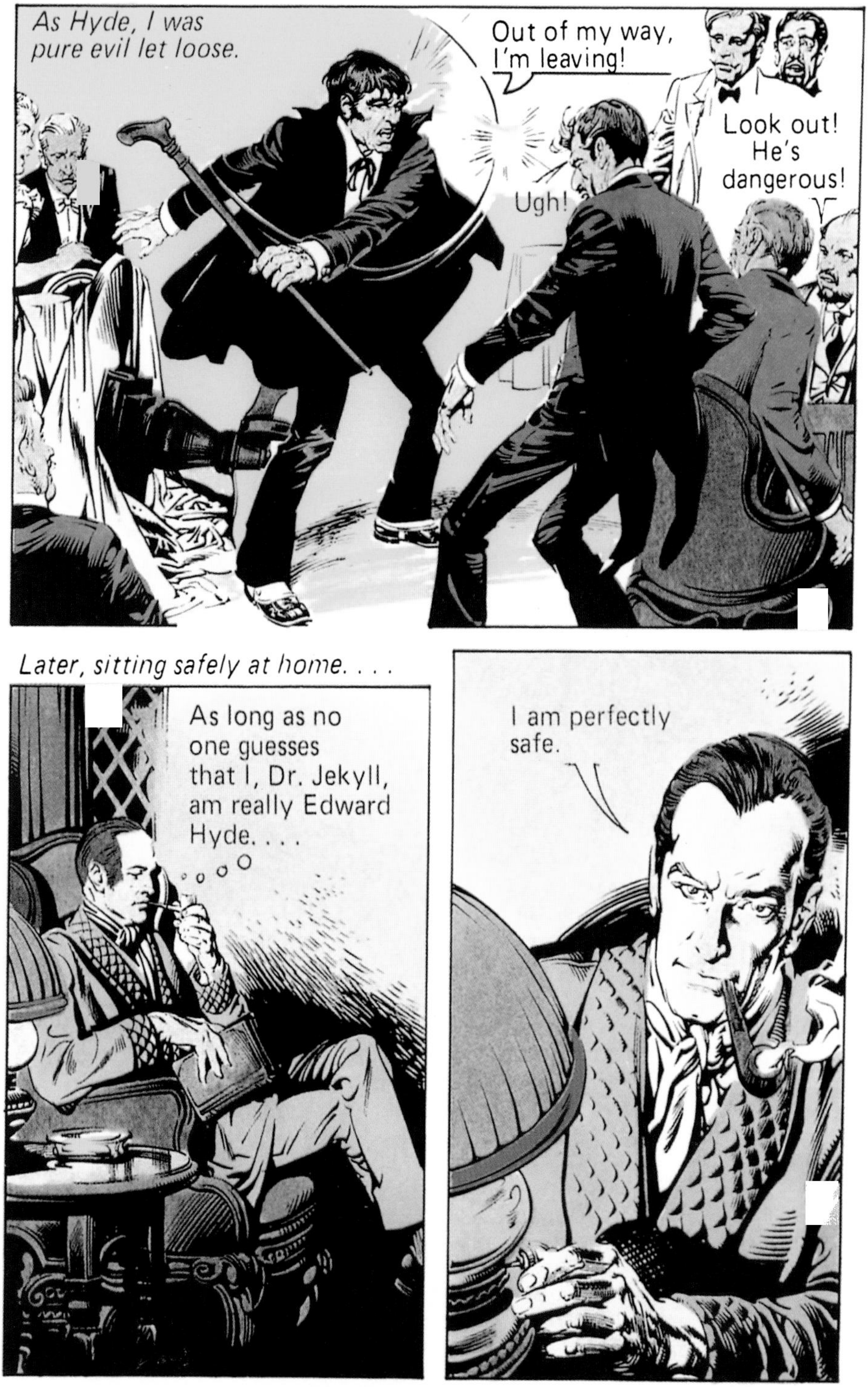
As Hyde, I was pure evil let loose.
Out of my way, I'm leaving!
Ugh!
Look out! He's dangerous!
Later, sitting safely at home. . . .
As long as no one guesses that I, Dr. Jekyll, am really Edward Hyde. . . .
I am perfectly safe.

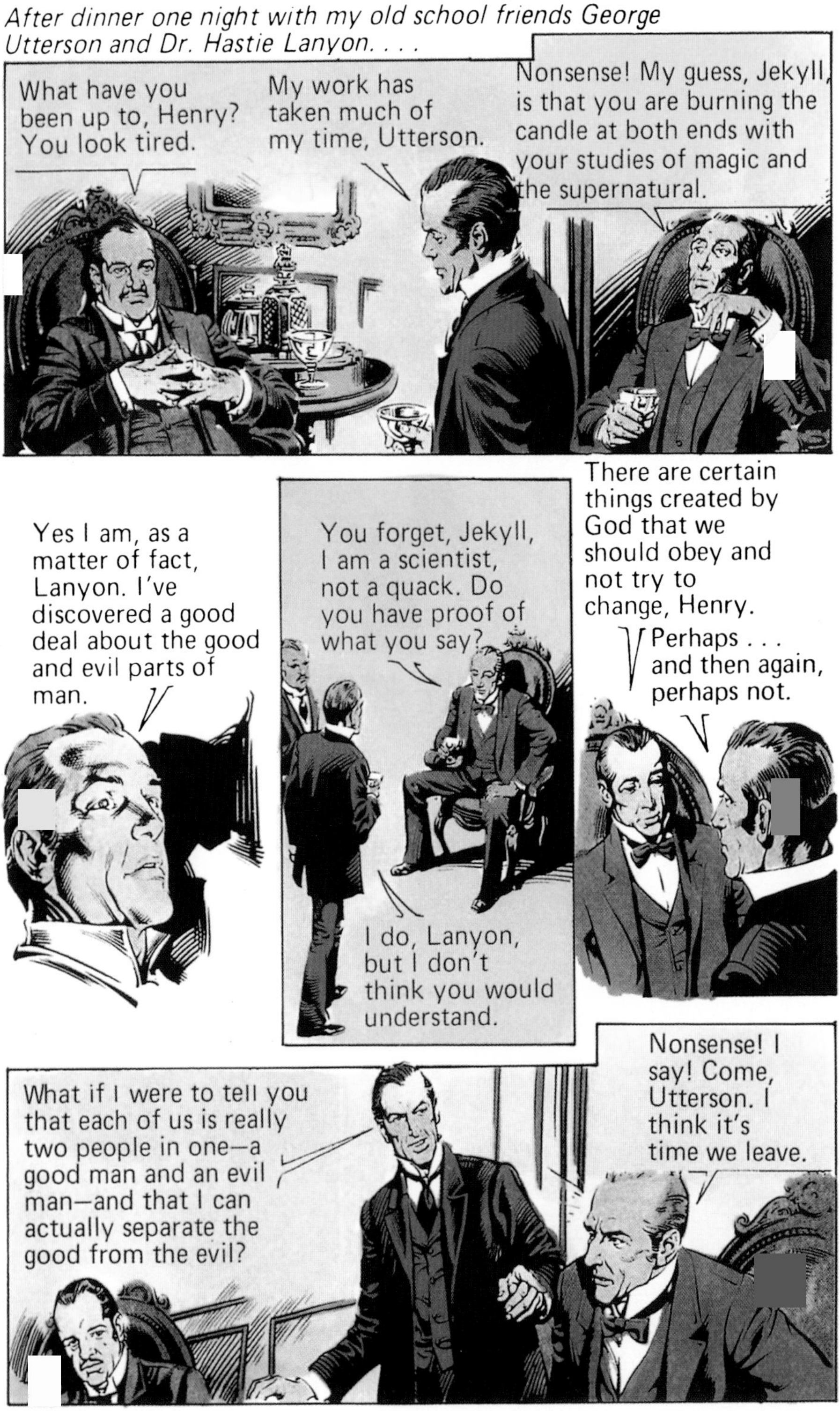
After dinner one night with my old school friends George Utterson and Dr. Hastie Lanyon. . . .
What have you been up to, Henry? You look tired.
My work has taken much of my time, Utterson.
Nonsense! My guess, Jekyll, is that you are burning the candle at both ends with your studies of magic and the supernatural.
Yes I am, as a matter of fact, Lanyon. I've discovered a good deal about the good and evil parts of man.
You forget, Jekyll, I am a scientist, not a quack. Do you have proof of what you say?
I do, Lanyon, but I don't think you would understand.
There are certain things created by God that we should obey and not try to change, Henry.
Perhaps . . . and then again, perhaps not.
What if I were to tell you that each of us is really two people in one—a good man and an evil man—and that I can actually separate the good from the evil?
Nonsense! I say! Come, Utterson. I think it's time we leave.

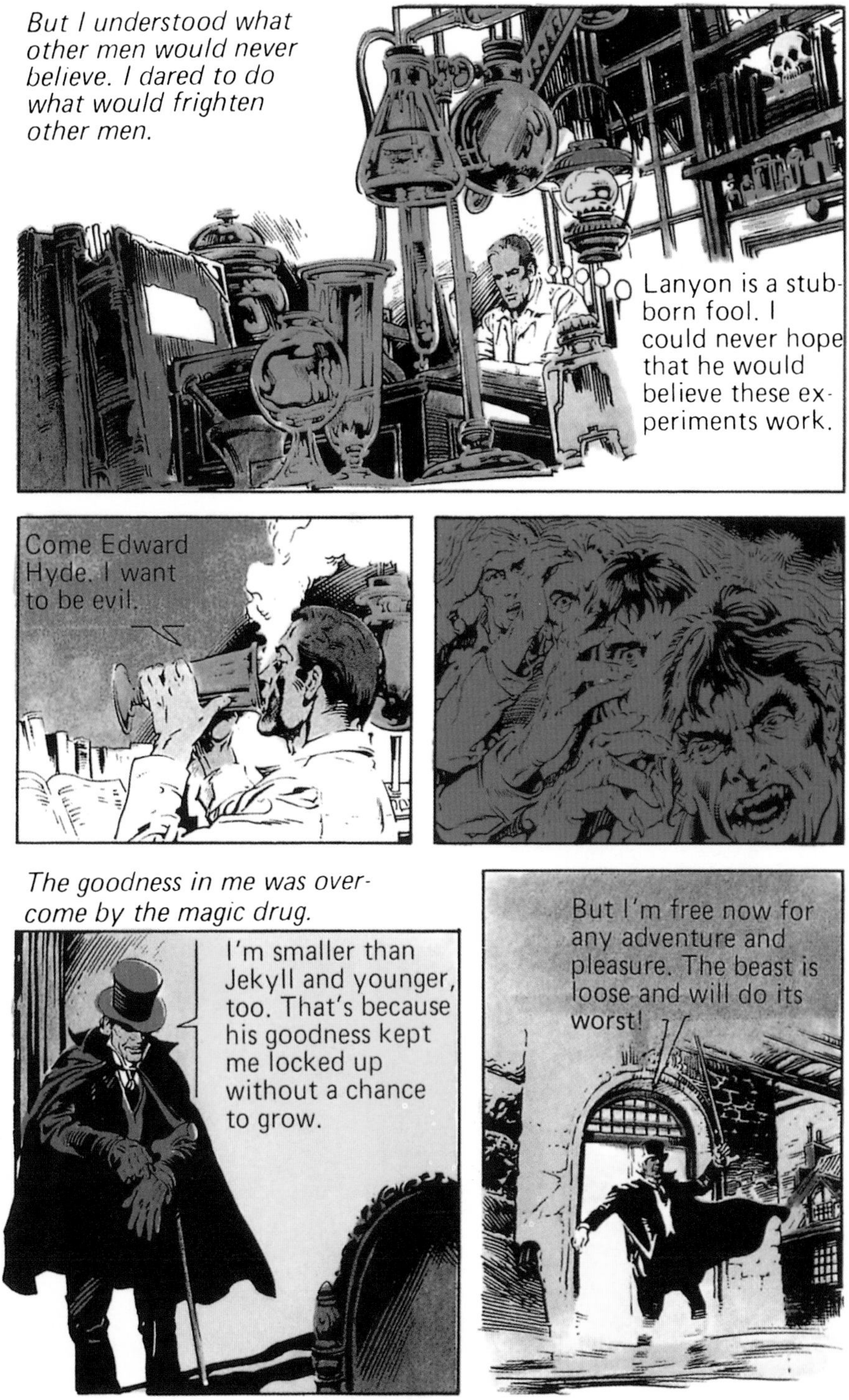
But I understood what other men would never believe. I dared to do what would frighten other men.
Lanyon is a stubborn fool. I could never hope that he would believe these experiments work.
Come Edward Hyde. I want to be evil.
The goodness in me was overcome by the magic drug.
I'm smaller than Jekyll and younger, too. That's because his goodness kept me locked up without a chance to grow.
But I'm free now for any adventure and pleasure. The beast is loose and will do its worst!

Again, as Hyde, a creature evil and wicked, I went after pleasure. Everything I did was for myself. I enjoyed hurting people. I was like a man of stone with no feelings.

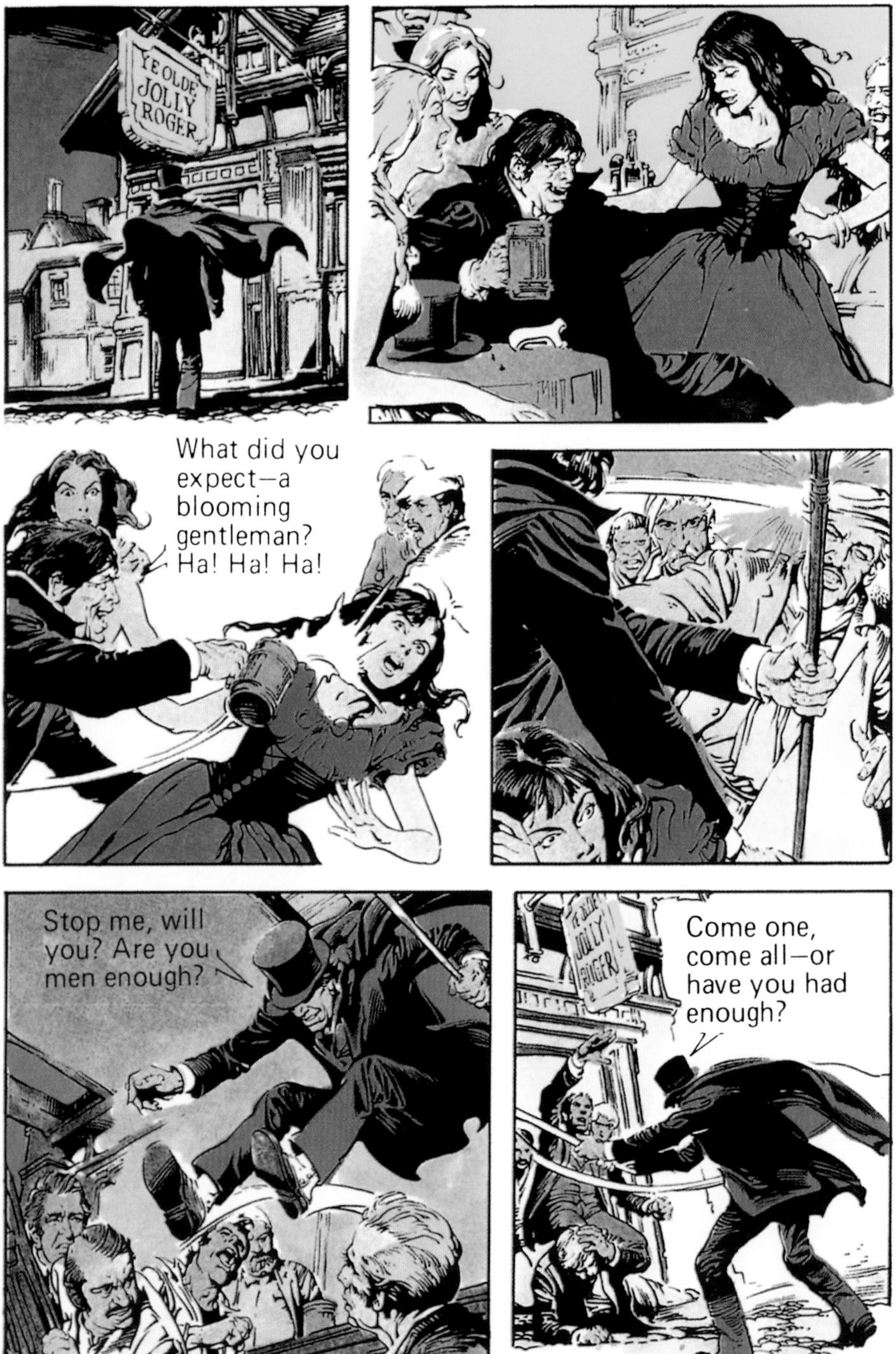
YE OLDE JOLLY ROGER
What did you expect—a blooming gentleman? Ha! Ha! Ha!
Stop me, will you? Are you men enough?
Come one, come all—or have you had enough?

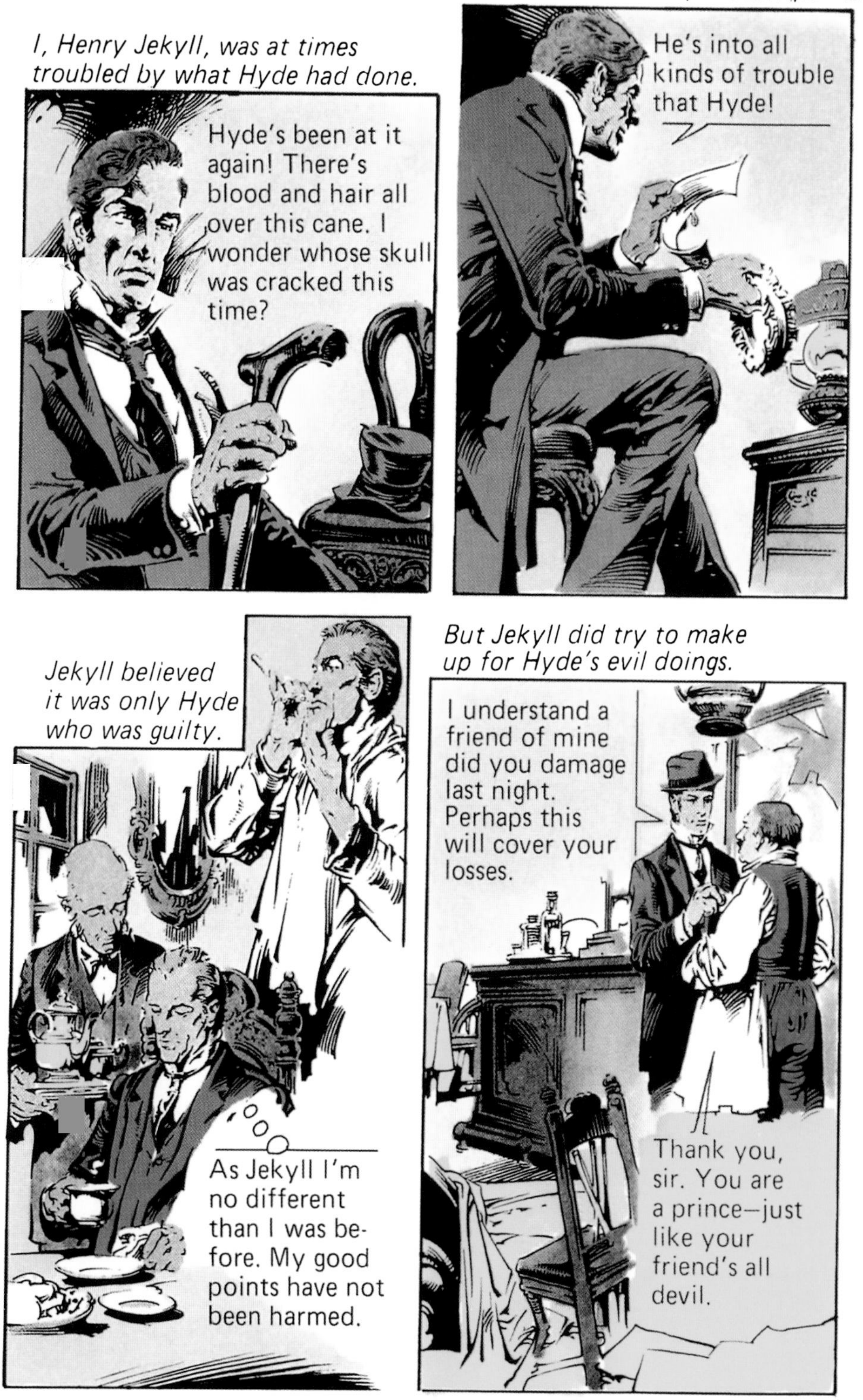
I, Henry Jekyll, was at times troubled by what Hyde had done.
Hyde's been at it again! There's blood and hair all over this cane. I wonder whose skull was cracked this time?
He's into all kinds of trouble that Hyde!
Jekyll believed it was only Hyde who was guilty.
As Jekyll I'm no different than I was before. My good points have not been harmed.
But Jekyll did try to make up for Hyde's evil doings.
I understand a friend of mine did you damage last night. Perhaps this will cover your losses.
Thank you, sir. You are a prince—just like your friend's all devil.

I had no idea of the trouble to come. . . .

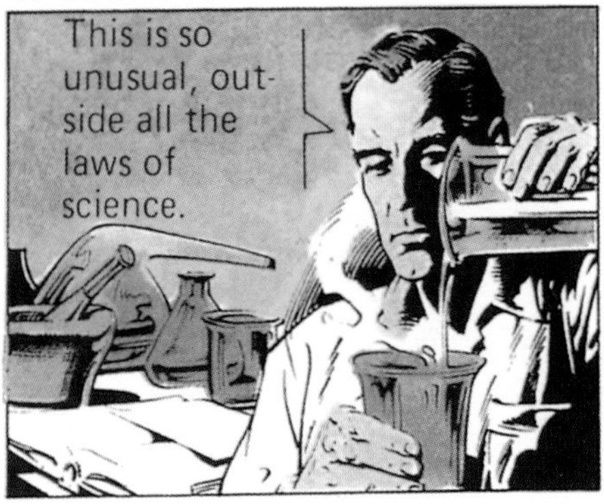
This is so unusual, outside all the laws of science.

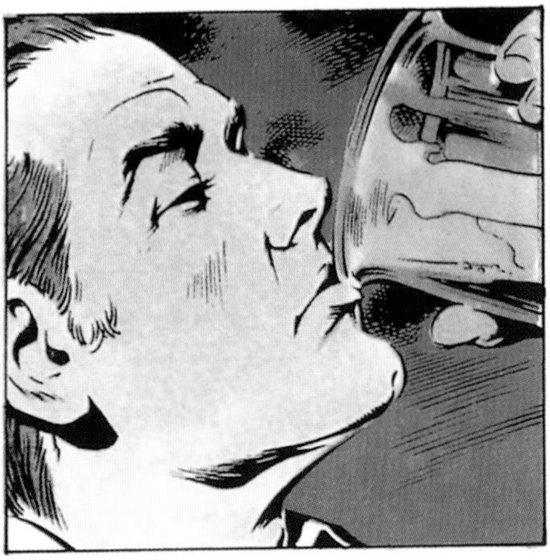

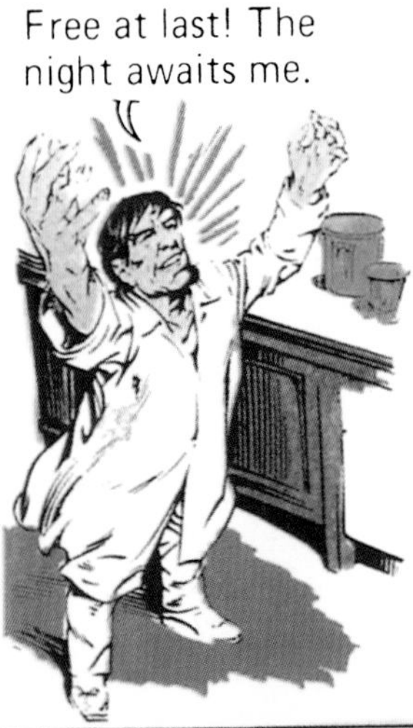
Free at last! The night awaits me.

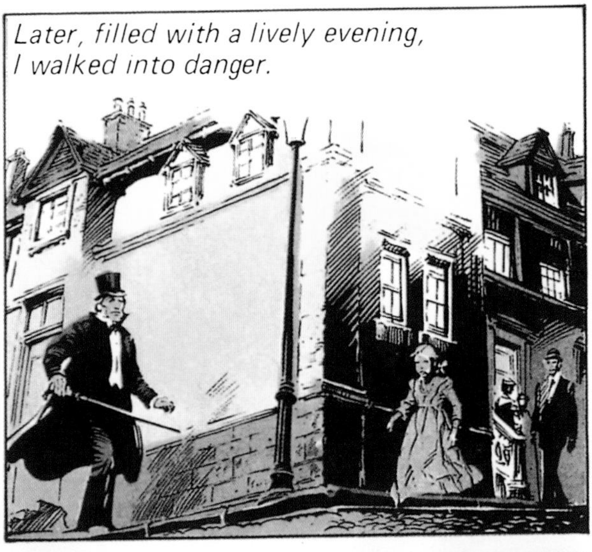
Later, filled with a lively evening, I walked into danger.

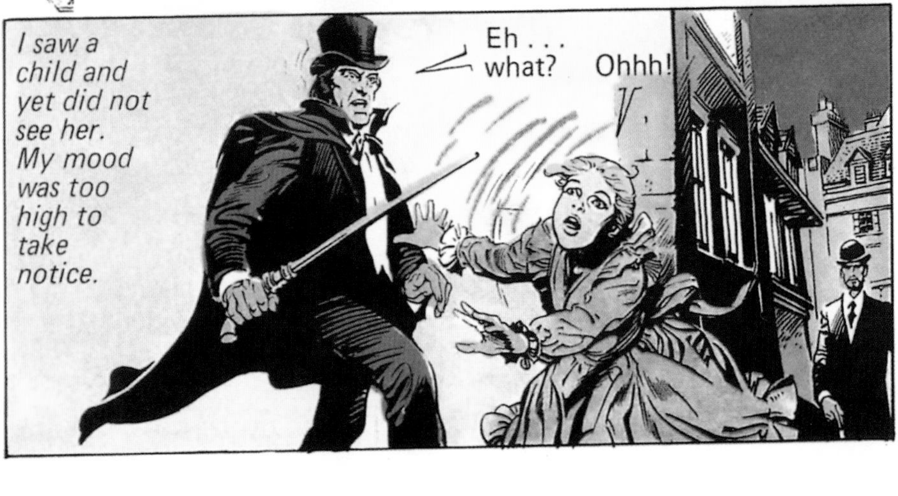
I saw a child and yet did not see her. My mood was too high to take notice.
Eh . . . what?
Ohhh!

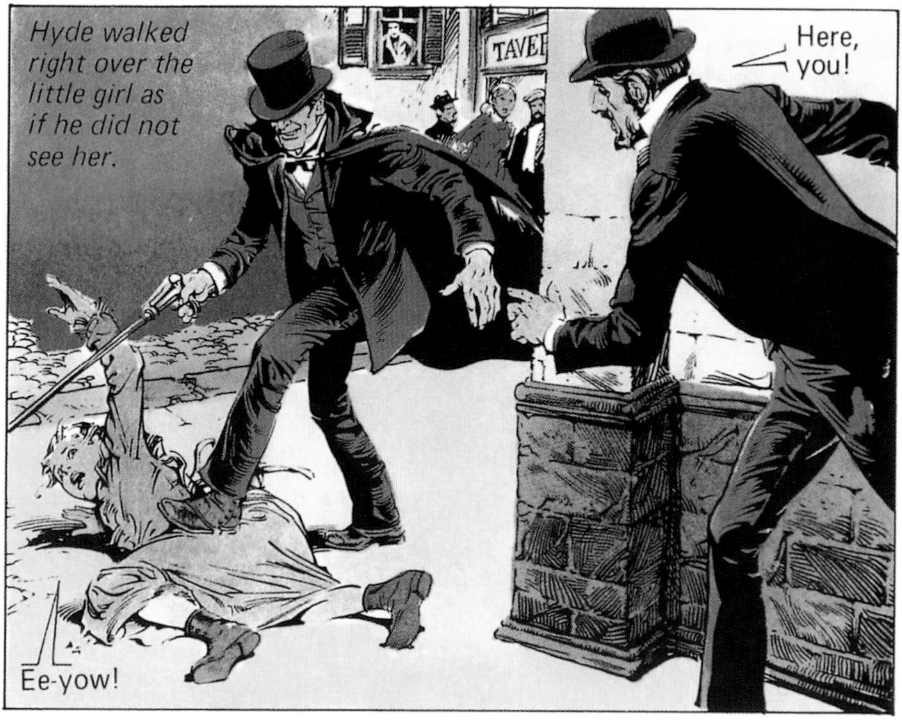
Hyde walked right over the little girl as if he did not see her.
TAVE
Here, you!
Ee-yow!

Only to be stopped by a man who saw the accident.

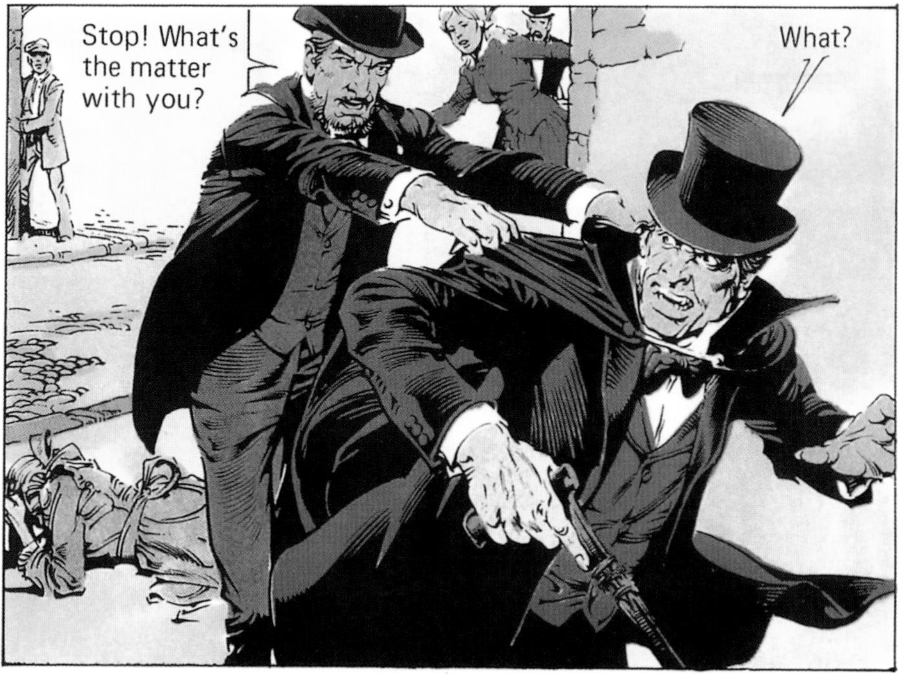
Stop! What's the matter with you?
What?

The accident with the child made her family and the whole neighborhood angry when they heard her cries.

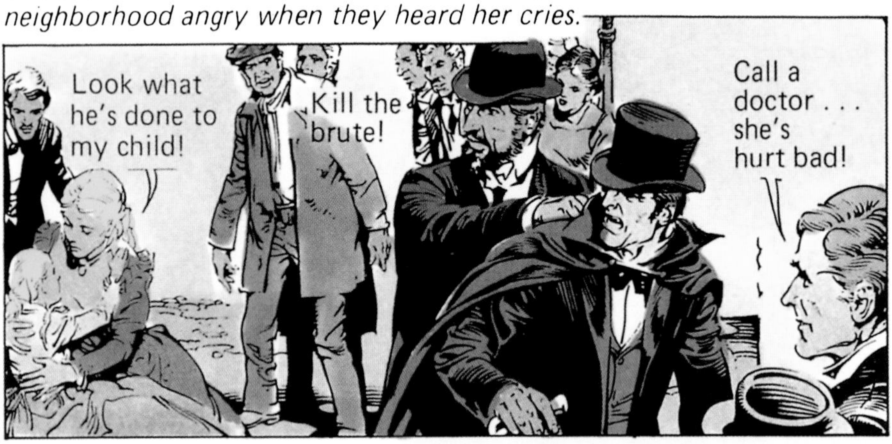
Look what he's done to my child!
Kill the brute!
Call a doctor . . . she's hurt bad!

Hyde knew he was in danger and acted quickly.

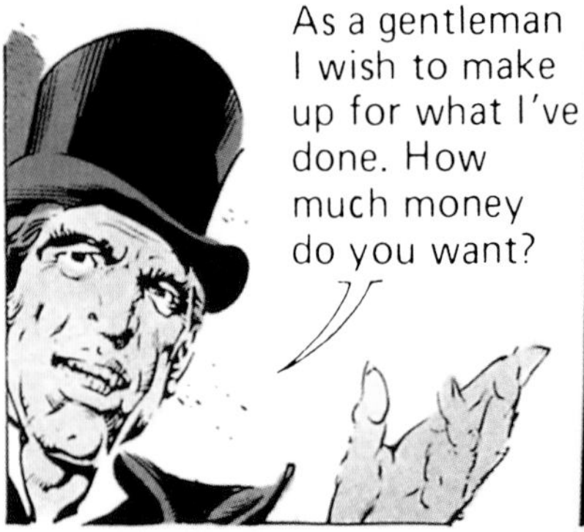
As a gentleman I wish to make up for what I've done. How much money do you want?

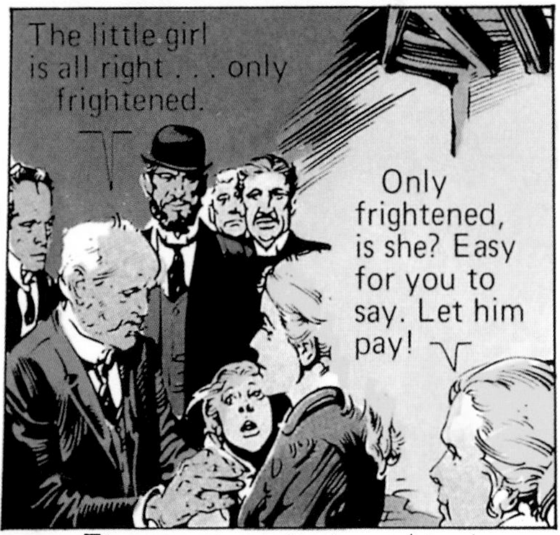
The little girl is all right . . . only frightened.
Only frightened, is she? Easy for you to say. Let him pay!

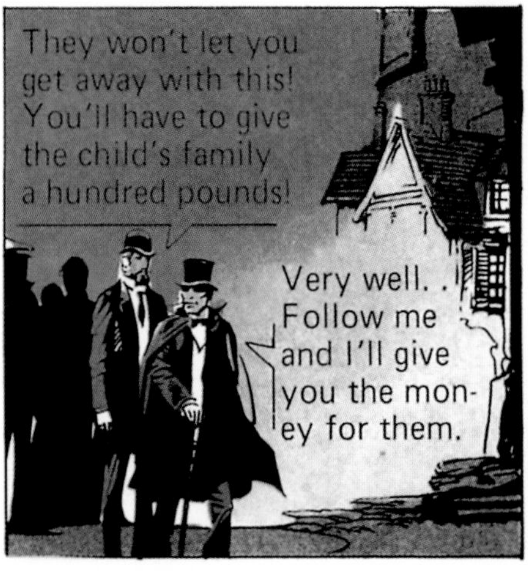
They won't let you get away with this! You'll have to give the child's family a hundred pounds!
Very well. . Follow me and I'll give you the mon-ey for them.

The people waited outside the door to Jekyll's laboratory as Hyde went in.

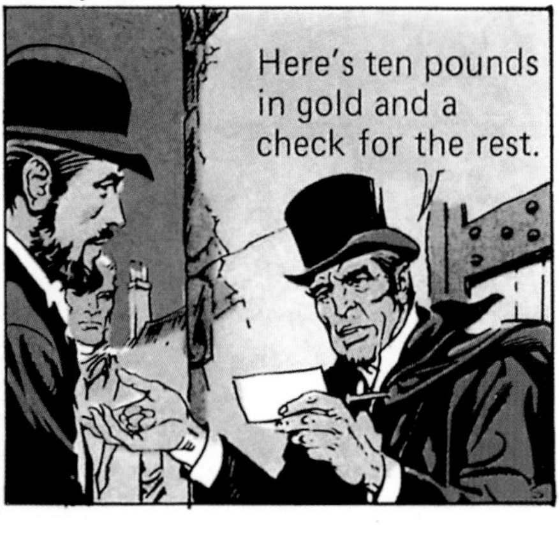
Here's ten pounds in gold and a check for the rest.

I knew the man who had grabbed me was a relative to Utterson, Jekyll's lawyer. He stared at the signature on the check.

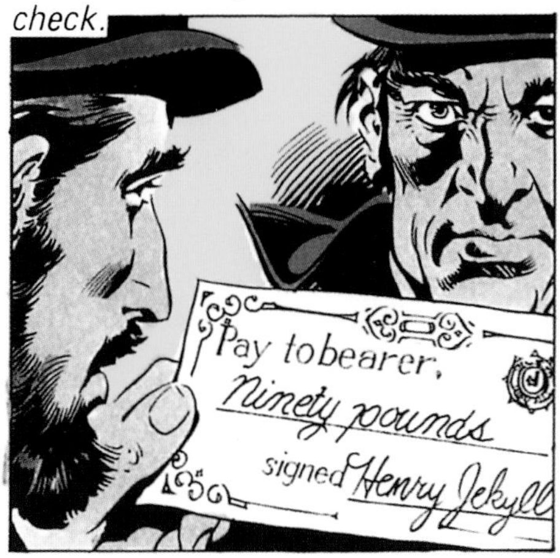
Pay to bearer,
Ninety pounds
signed Henry Jekyll

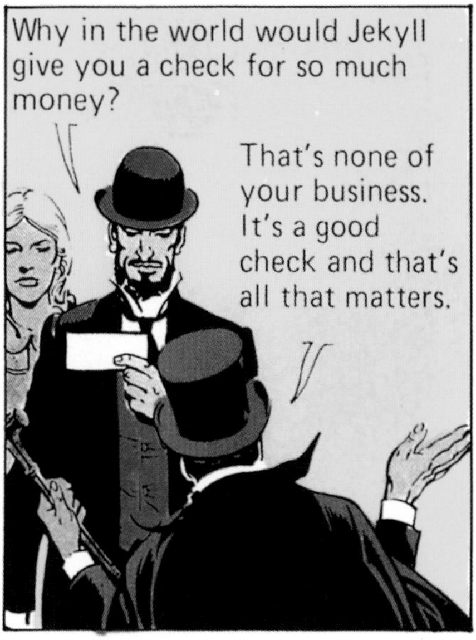
Why in the world would Jekyll give you a check for so much money?
That's none of your business. It's a good check and that's all that matters.

I knew I had to get a bank account in the name of Edward Hyde.

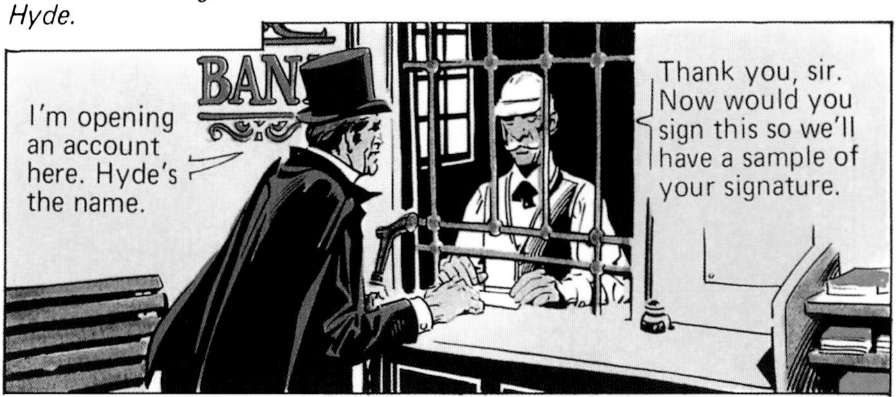
I'm opening an account here. Hyde's the name.
Thank you, sir. Now would you sign this so we'll have a sample of your signature.

I changed my signature by slanting my handwriting backwards.

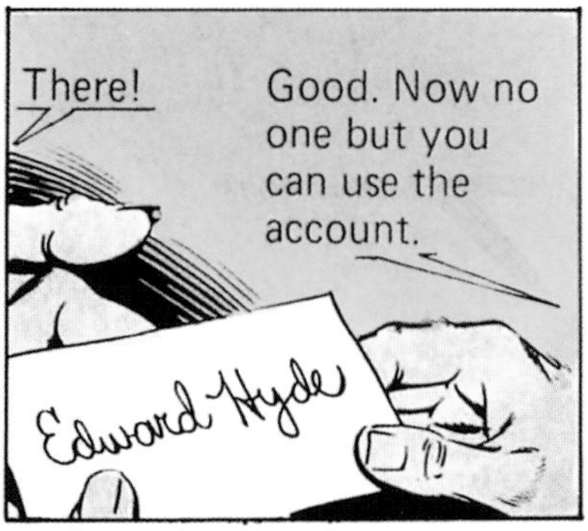
There!
Good. Now no one but you can use the account.
Edward Hyde

I thought I was safe.

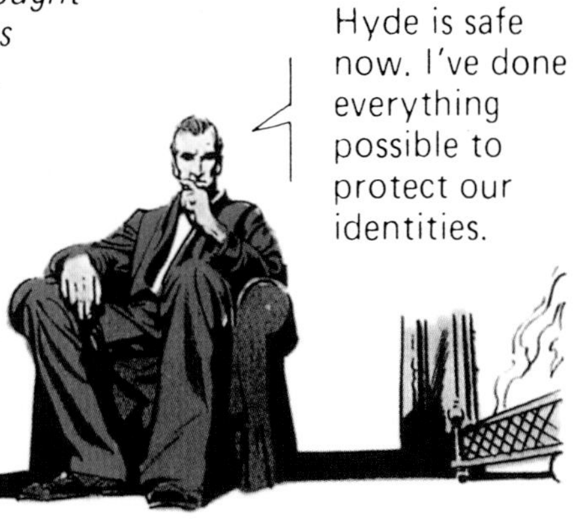
Hyde is safe now. I've done everything possible to protect our identities.

One day my friend and lawyer, George Utterson, was walking with his relative Mr. Enfield.

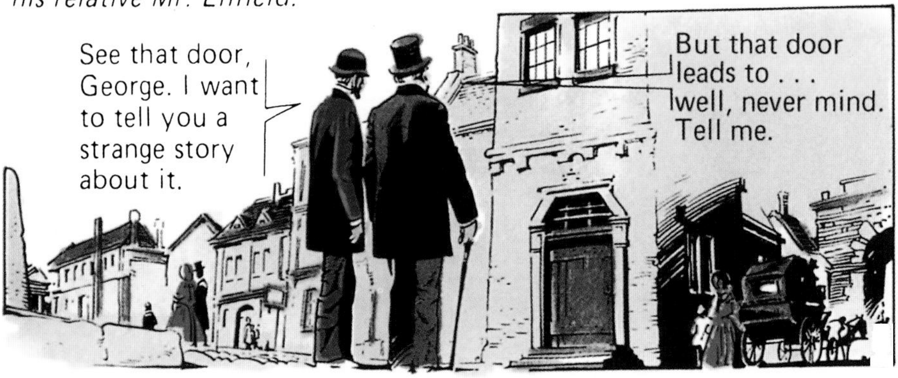
See that door, George. I want to tell you a strange story about it.
But that door leads to . . . well, never mind. Tell me.

Enfield then told the story of Hyde's accident with the girl.

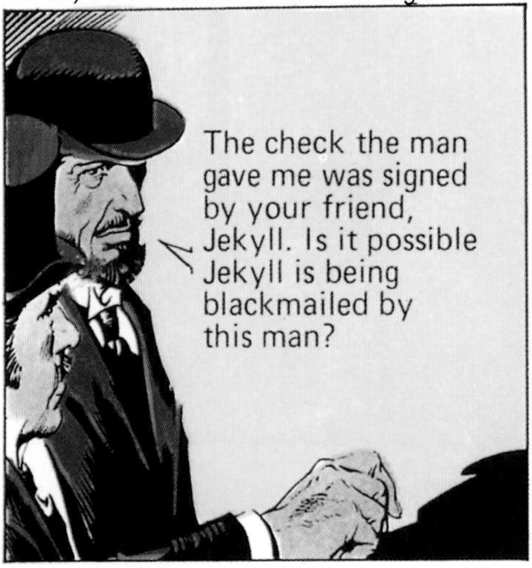
The check the man gave me was signed by your friend, Jekyll. Is it possible Jekyll is being blackmailed by this man?

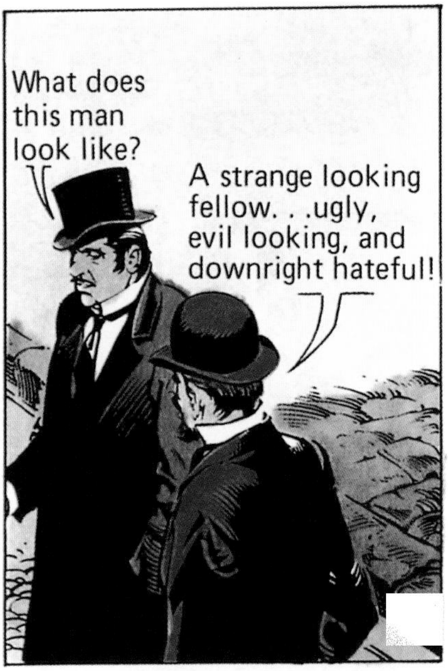
What does this man look like?
A strange looking fellow. . .ugly, evil looking, and downright hateful!

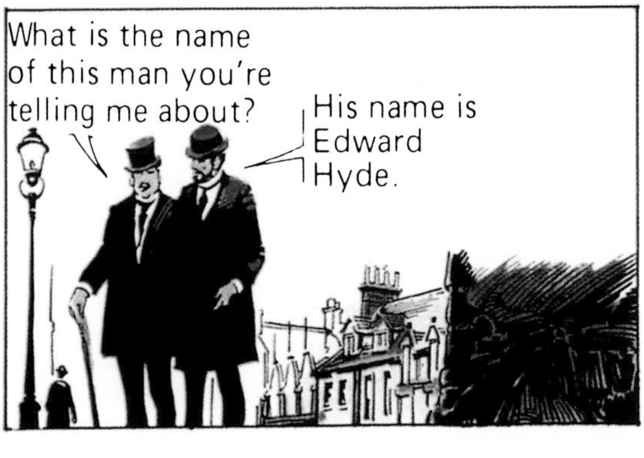
What is the name of this man you're telling me about?
His name is Edward Hyde.

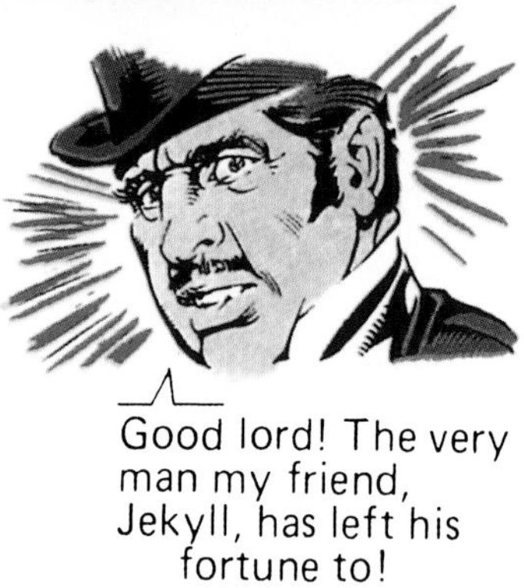
Good lord! The very man my friend, Jekyll, has left his fortune to!

Utterson went home sadly when Enfield told him Hyde had his own key to Jekyll's door.

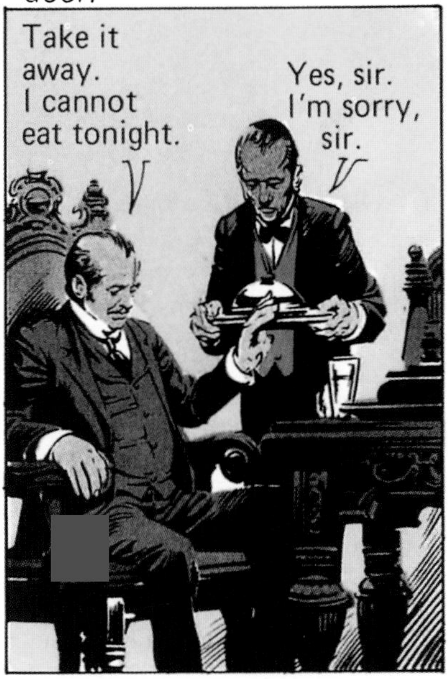
Take it away. I cannot eat tonight.
Yes, sir. I'm sorry, sir.

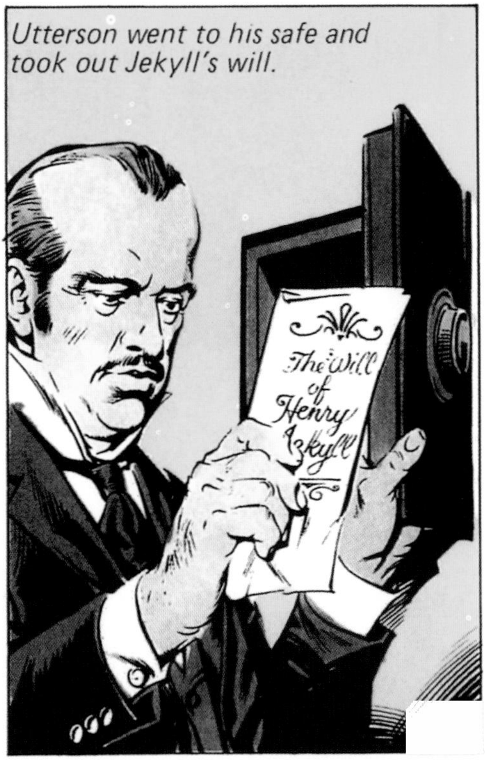
Utterson went to his safe and took out Jekyll's will.
The Will of Henry Jekyll

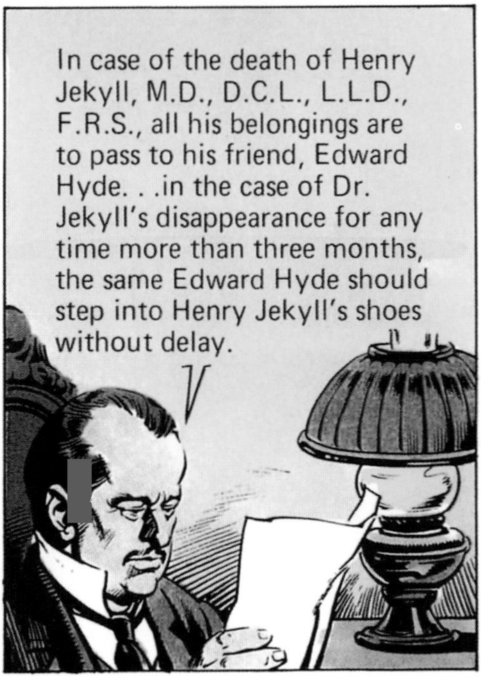
In case of the death of Henry Jekyll, M.D., D.C.L., L.L.D., F.R.S., all his belongings are to pass to his friend, Edward Hyde. . .in the case of Dr. Jekyll's disappearance for any time more than three months, the same Edward Hyde should step into Henry Jekyll's shoes without delay.

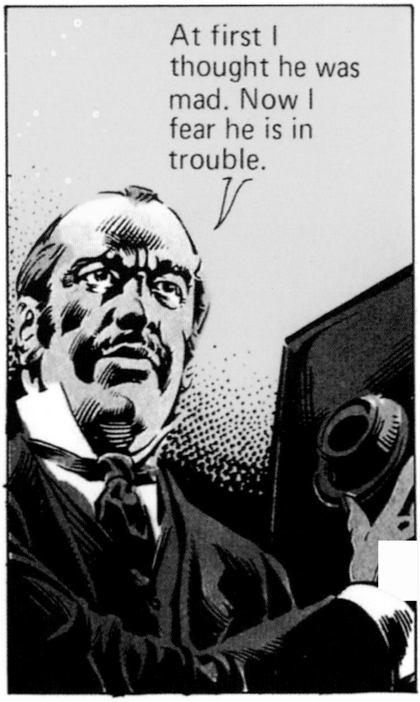
At first I thought he was mad. Now I fear he is in trouble.

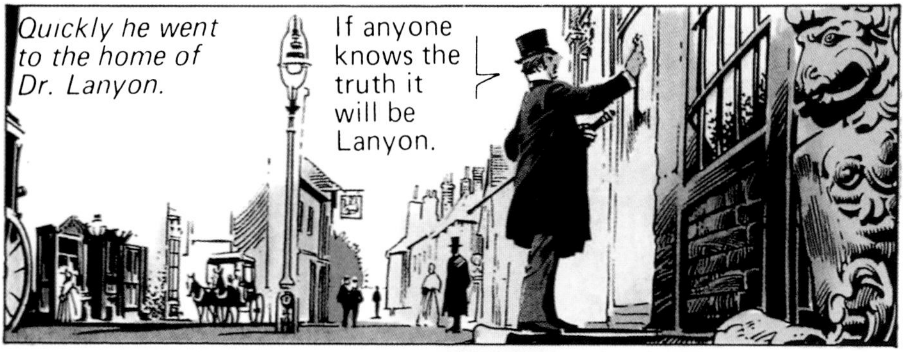
Quickly he went to the home of Dr. Lanyon.
If anyone knows the truth it will be Lanyon.

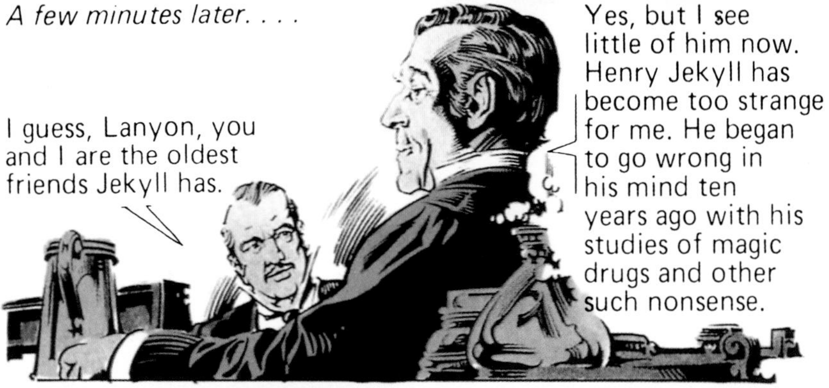
A few minutes later. . . .
I guess, Lanyon, you and I are the oldest friends Jekyll has.
Yes, but I see little of him now. Henry Jekyll has become too strange for me. He began to go wrong in his mind ten years ago with his studies of magic drugs and other such nonsense.

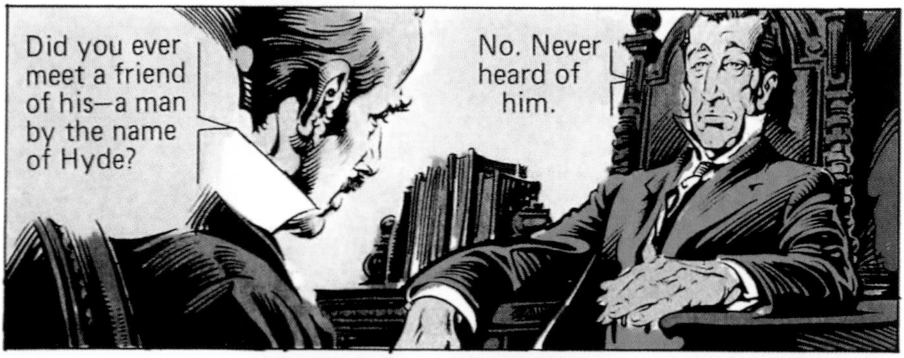
Did you ever meet a friend of his—a man by the name of Hyde?
No. Never heard of him.

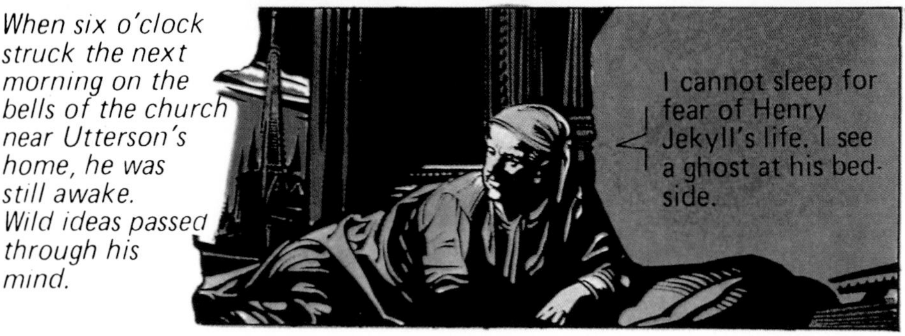
When six o'clock struck the next morning on the bells of the church near Utterson's home, he was still awake. Wild ideas passed through his mind.
I cannot sleep for fear of Henry Jekyll's life. I see a ghost at his bed-side.

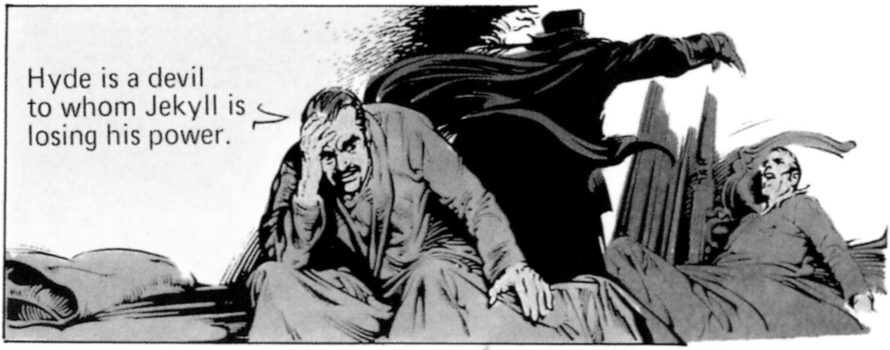
Hyde is a devil to whom Jekyll is losing his power.

The ghost of Hyde continued to fill Utterson's dreams.

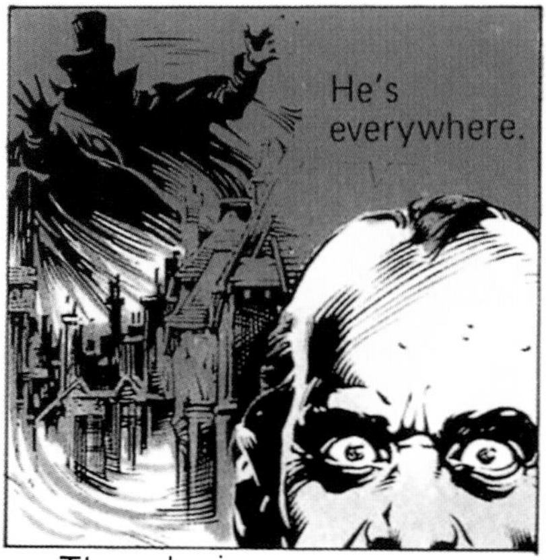
He's everywhere.

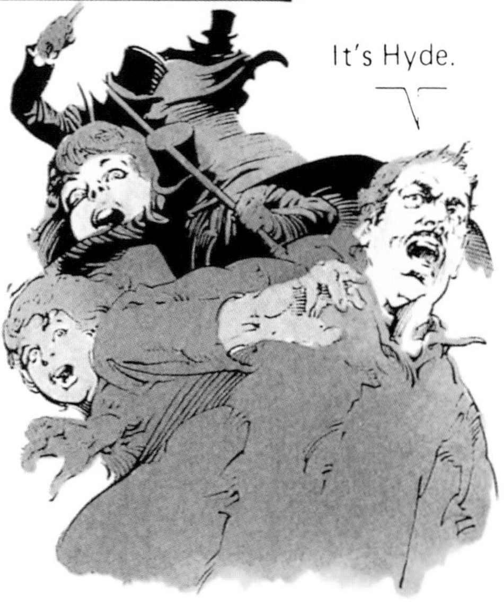
It's Hyde.

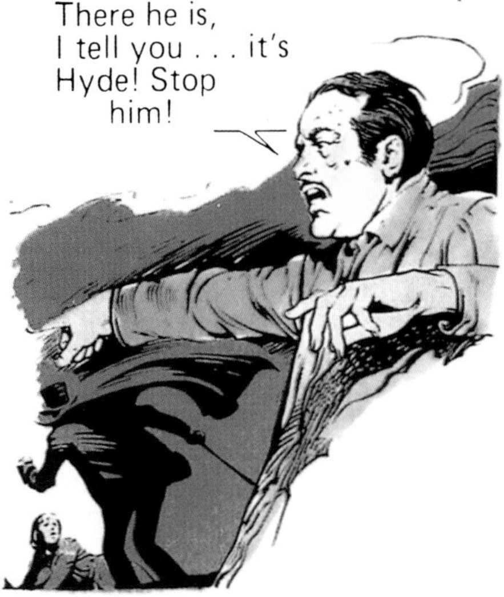
There he is, I tell you . . . it's Hyde! Stop him!

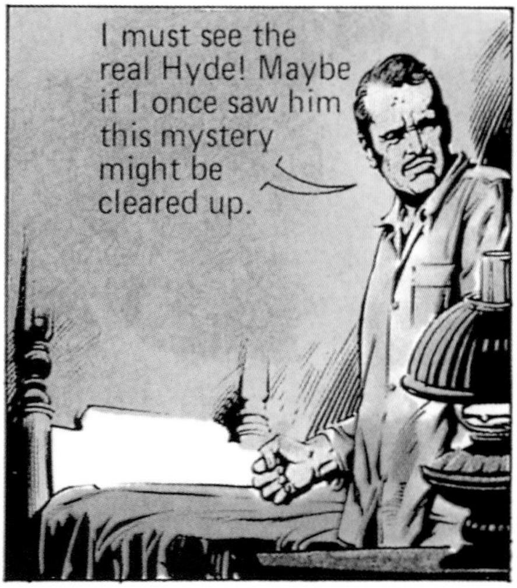
I must see the real Hyde! Maybe if I once saw him this mystery might be cleared up.

The mystery of Hyde made Utterson watch the door to Jekyll's laboratory from morning to night.

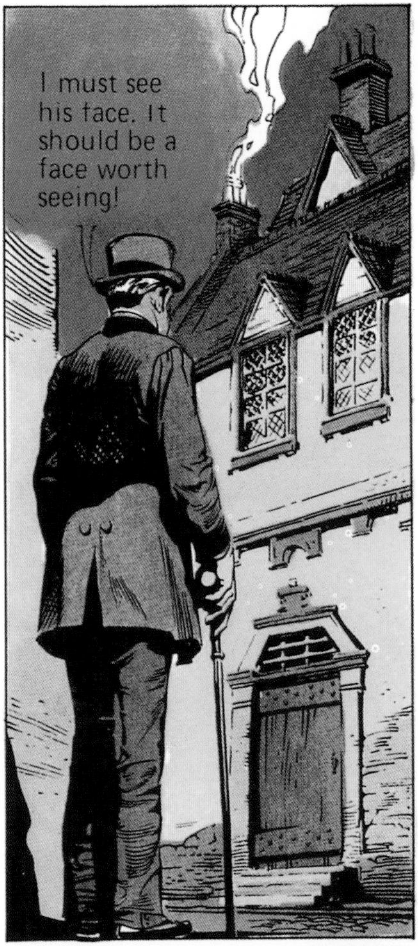
I must see his face. It should be a face worth seeing!

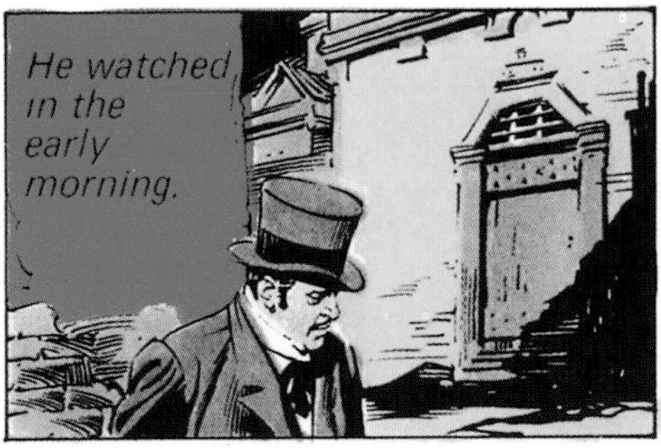
He watched in the early morning.

He watched at noon when the streets were busy.

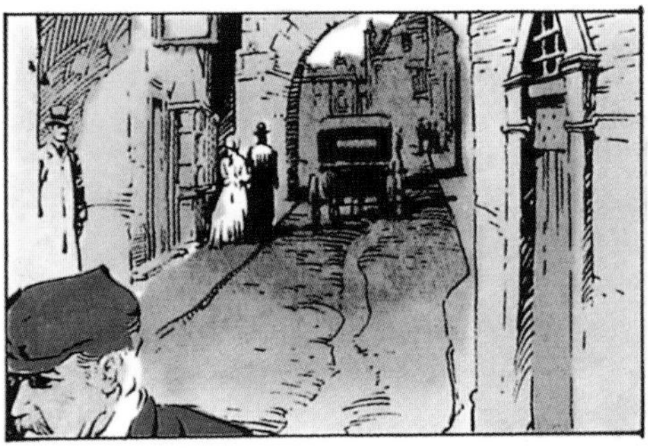

He watched at night under the face of the moon.

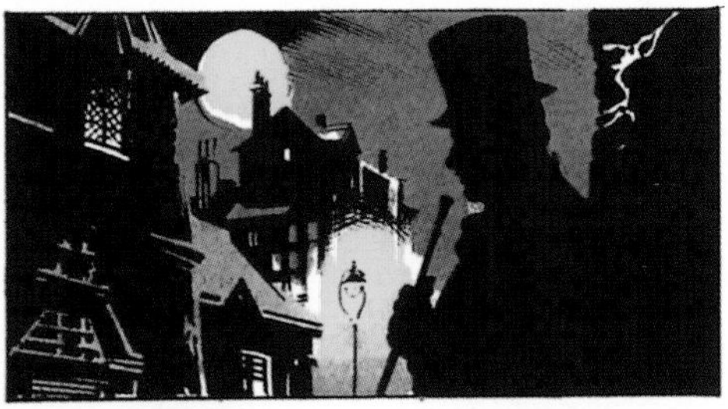

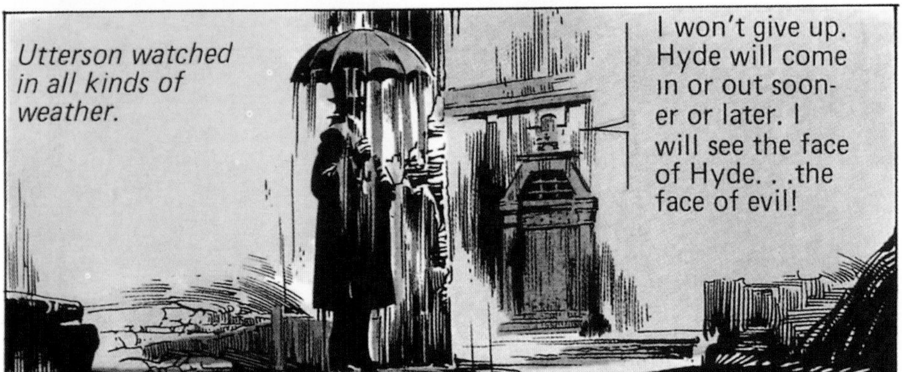
Utterson watched in all kinds of weather.
I won't give up. Hyde will come in or out sooner or later. I will see the face of Hyde. . .the face of evil!

Finally. . . .

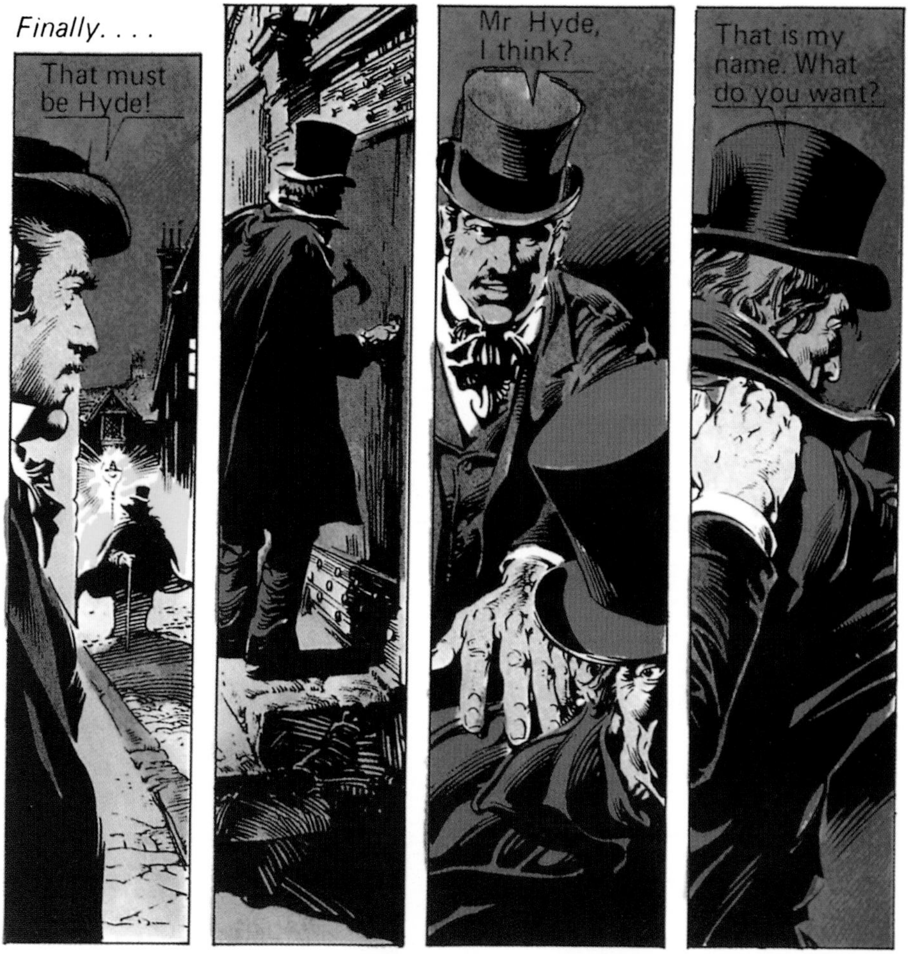
That must be Hyde!
Mr Hyde, I think?
That is my name. What do you want?

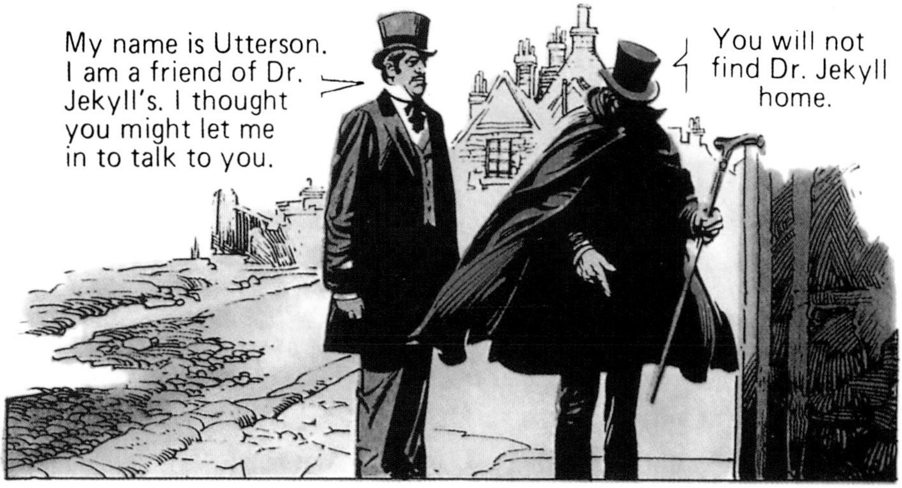
My name is Utterson. I am a friend of Dr. Jekyll's. I thought you might let me in to talk to you.
You will not find Dr. Jekyll home.

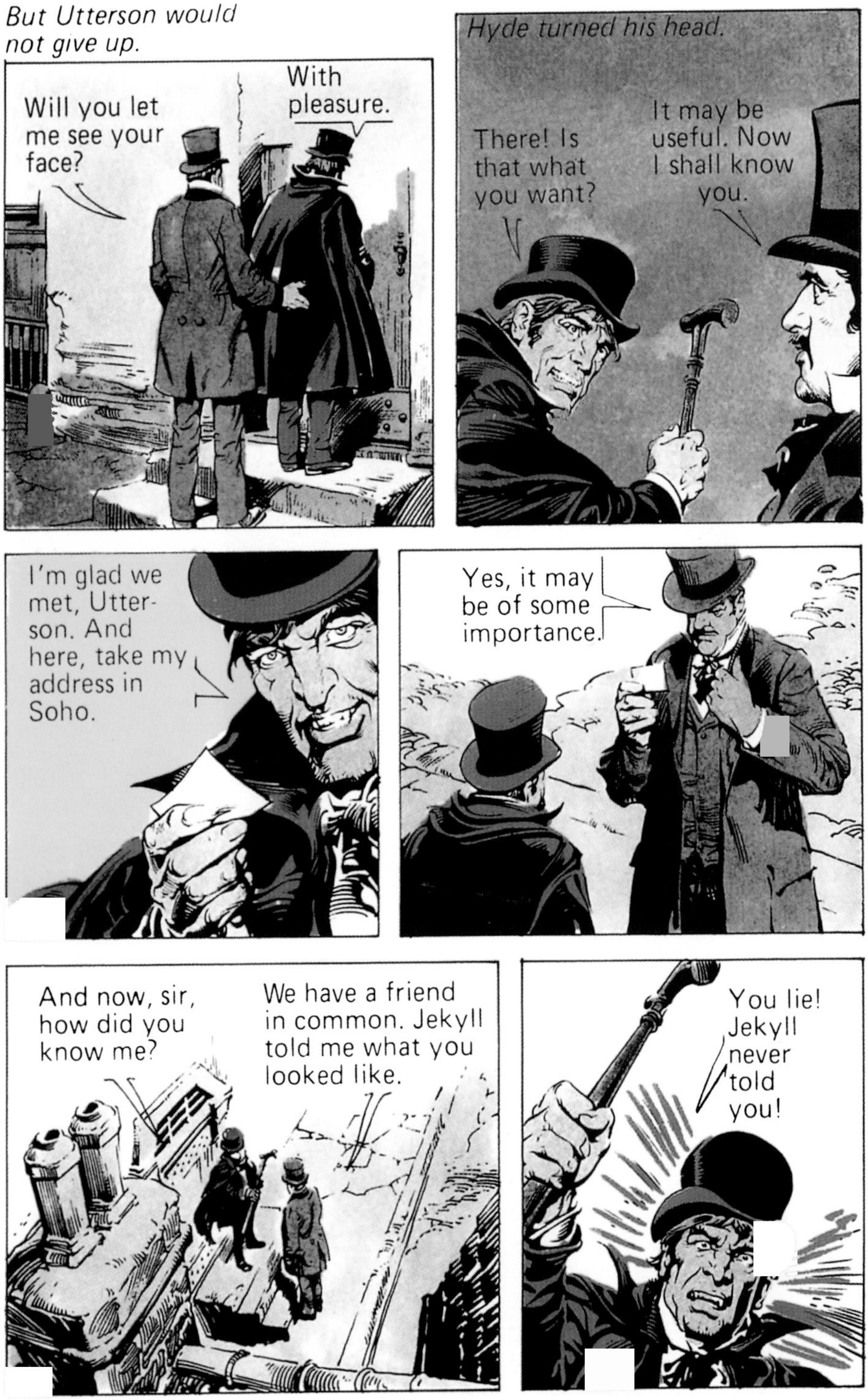
But Utterson would not give up.
Will you let me see your face?
With pleasure.
Hyde turned his head.
There! Is that what you want?
It may be useful. Now I shall know you.
I'm glad we met, Utter-son. And here, take my address in Soho.
Yes, it may be of some importance.
And now, sir, how did you know me?
We have a friend in common. Jekyll told me what you looked like.
You lie! Jekyll never told you!

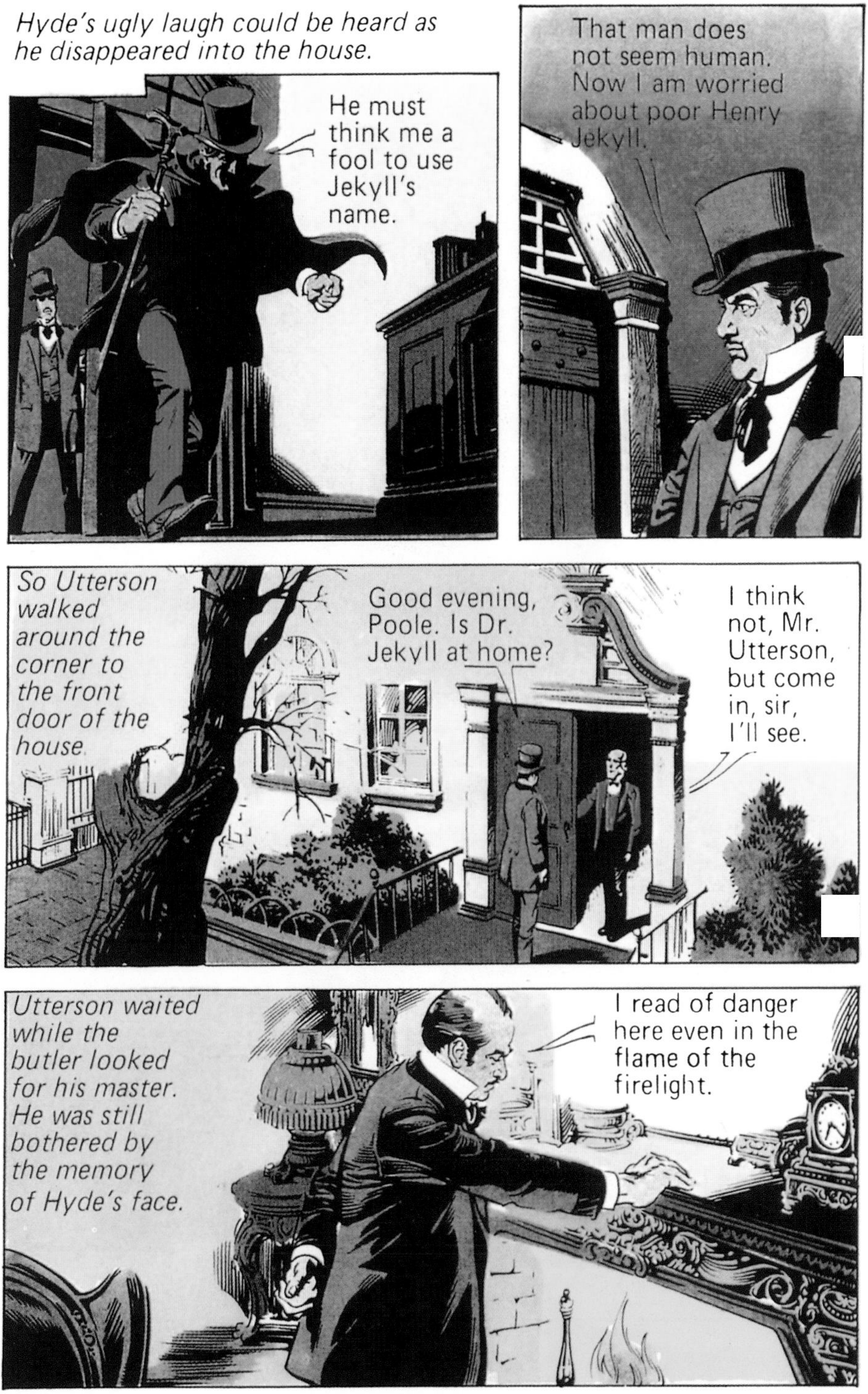
Hyde's ugly laugh could be heard as he disappeared into the house.
He must think me a fool to use Jekyll's name.
That man does not seem human. Now I am worried about poor Henry Jekyll.
So Utterson walked around the corner to the front door of the house.
Good evening, Poole. Is Dr. Jekyll at home?
I think not, Mr. Utterson, but come in, sir, I'll see.
Utterson waited while the butler looked for his master. He was still bothered by the memory of Hyde's face.
I read of danger here even in the flame of the firelight.

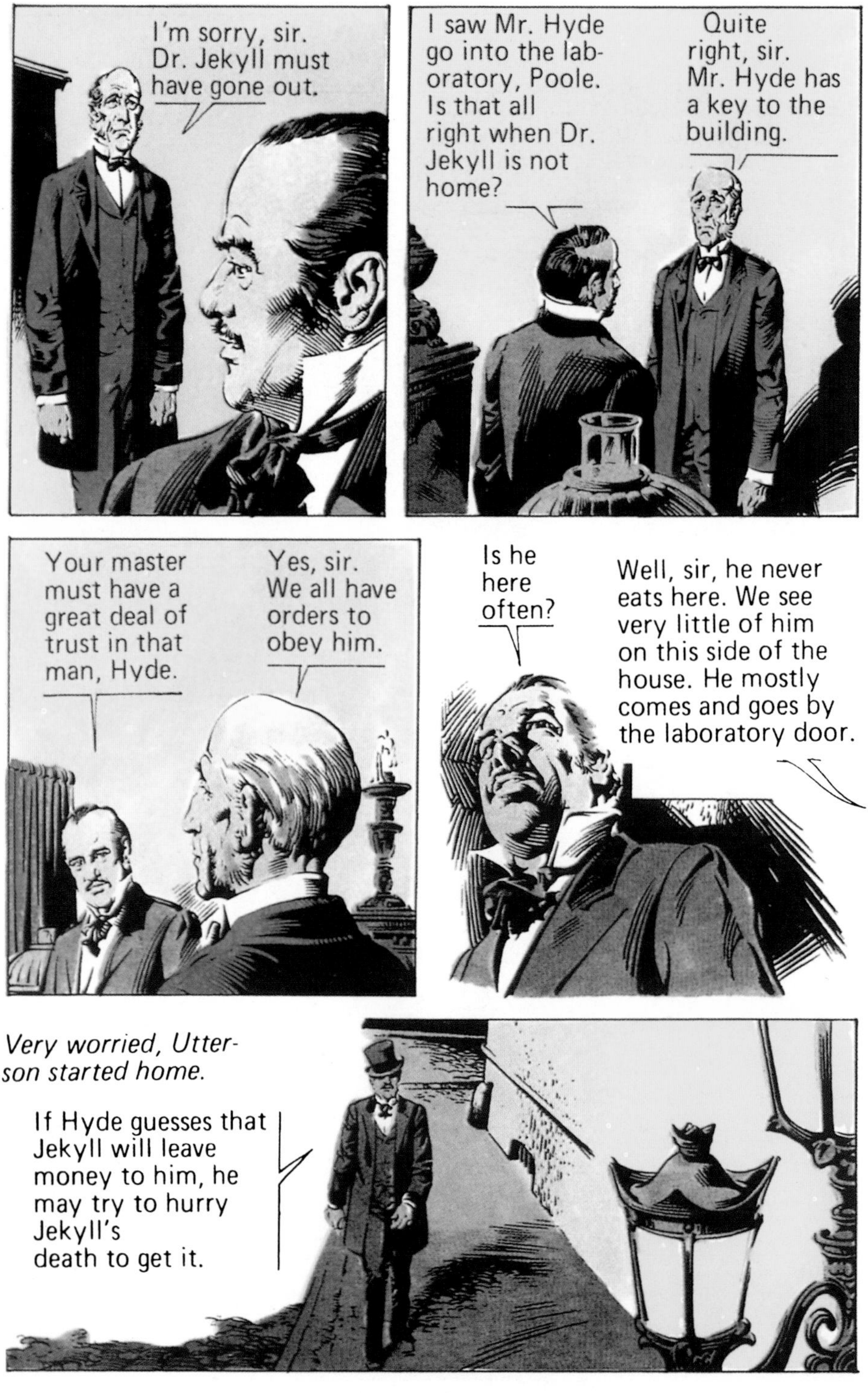
I'm sorry, sir. Dr. Jekyll must have gone out.
I saw Mr. Hyde go into the laboratory, Poole. Is that all right when Dr. Jekyll is not home?
Quite right, sir. Mr. Hyde has a key to the building.
Your master must have a great deal of trust in that man, Hyde.
Yes, sir. We all have orders to obey him.
Is he here often?
Well, sir, he never eats here. We see very little of him on this side of the house. He mostly comes and goes by the laboratory door.
Very worried, Utterson started home.
If Hyde guesses that Jekyll will leave money to him, he may try to hurry Jekyll's death to get it.

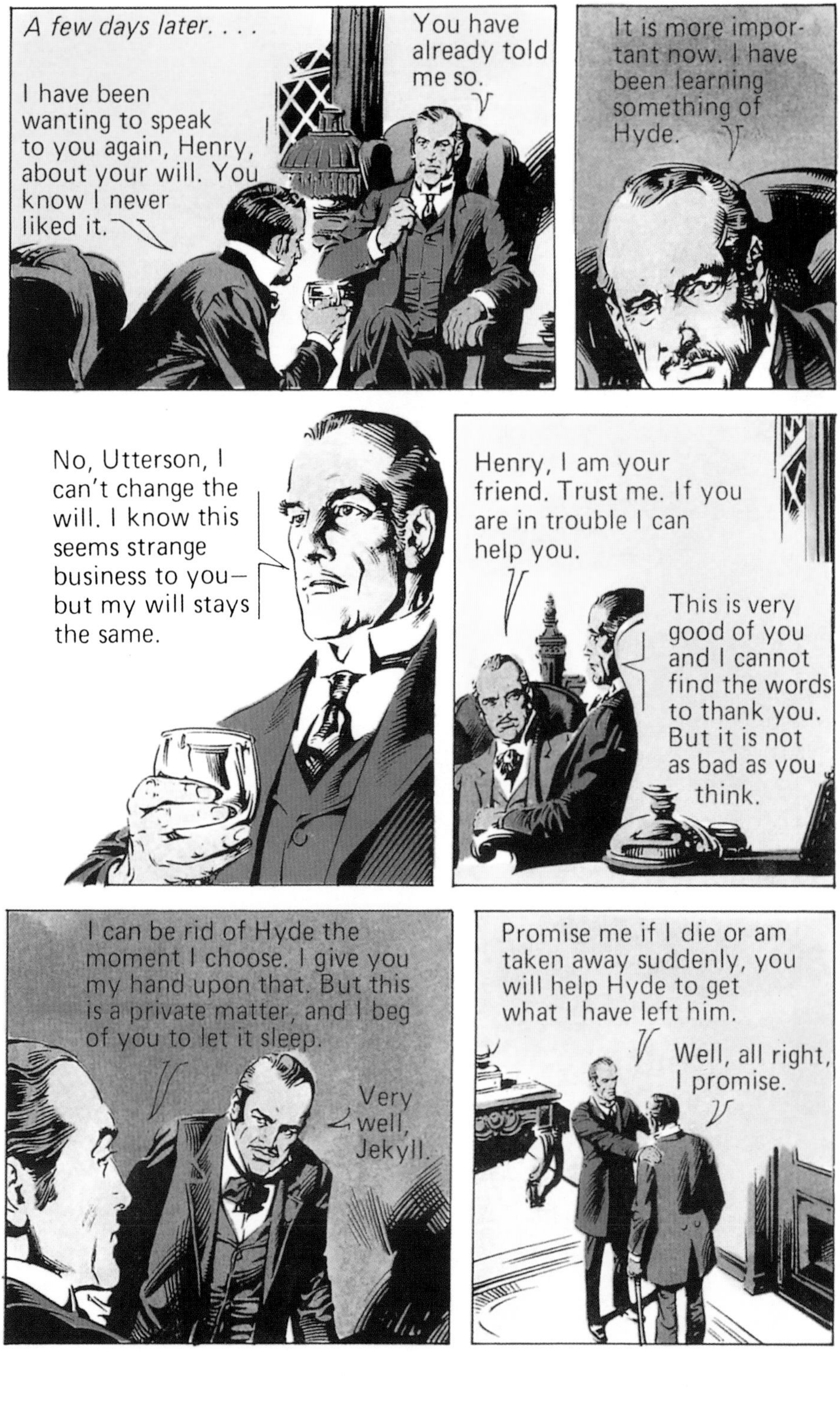
A few days later. . . .
I have been wanting to speak to you again, Henry, about your will. You know I never liked it.
You have already told me so.
It is more important now. I have been learning something of Hyde.
No, Utterson, I can't change the will. I know this seems strange business to you—but my will stays the same.
Henry, I am your friend. Trust me. If you are in trouble I can help you.
This is very good of you and I cannot find the words to thank you. But it is not as bad as you think.
I can be rid of Hyde the moment I choose. I give you my hand upon that. But this is a private matter, and I beg of you to let it sleep.
Very well, Jekyll.
Promise me if I die or am taken away suddenly, you will help Hyde to get what I have left him.
Well, all right, I promise.

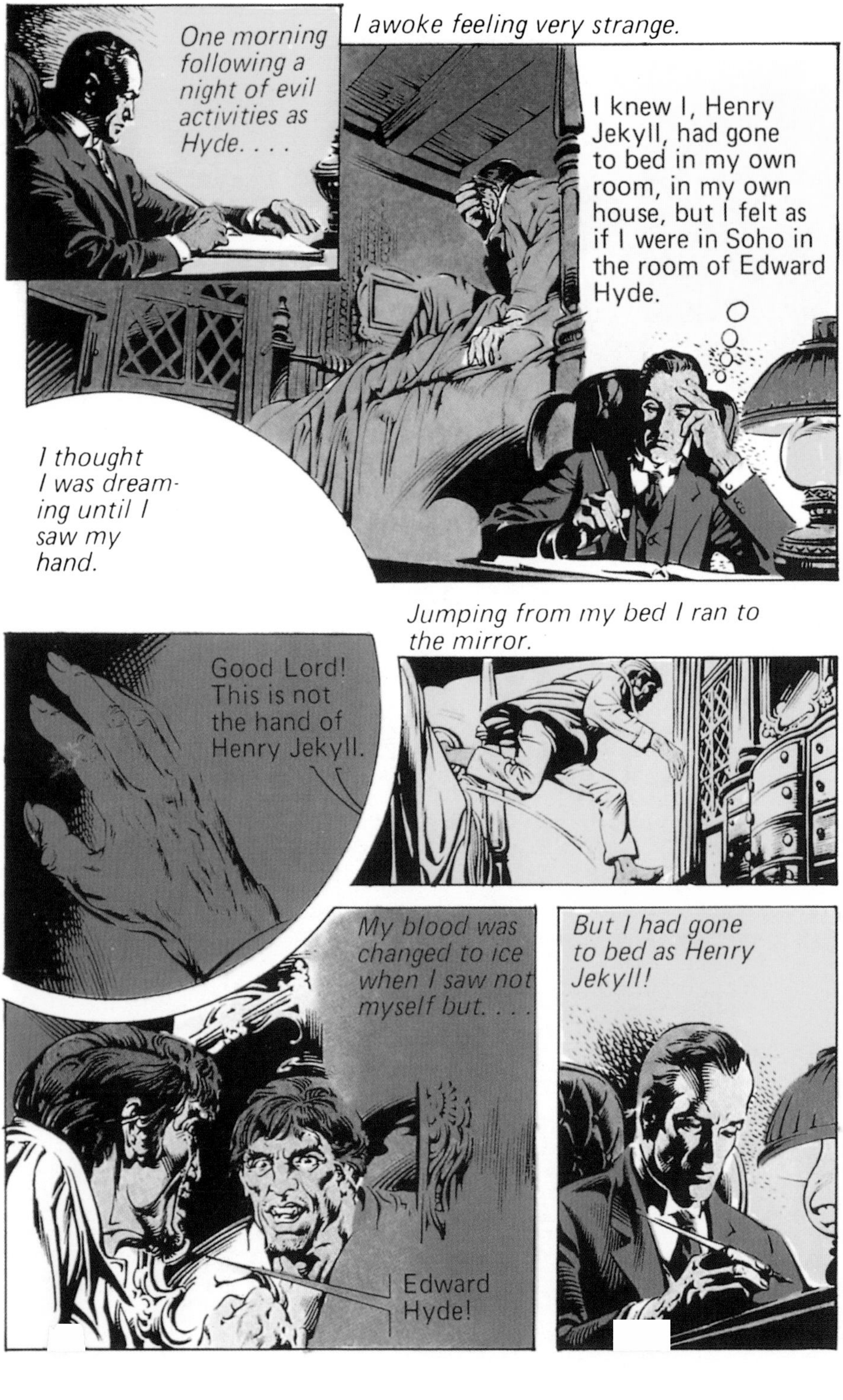
One morning following a night of evil activities as Hyde. . . .
I awoke feeling very strange.
I knew I, Henry Jekyll, had gone to bed in my own room, in my own house, but I felt as if I were in Soho in the room of Edward Hyde.
I thought I was dream-ing until I saw my hand.
Good Lord! This is not the hand of Henry Jekyll.
Jumping from my bed I ran to the mirror.
My blood was changed to ice when I saw not myself but. . . .
Edward Hyde!
But I had gone to bed as Henry Jekyll!

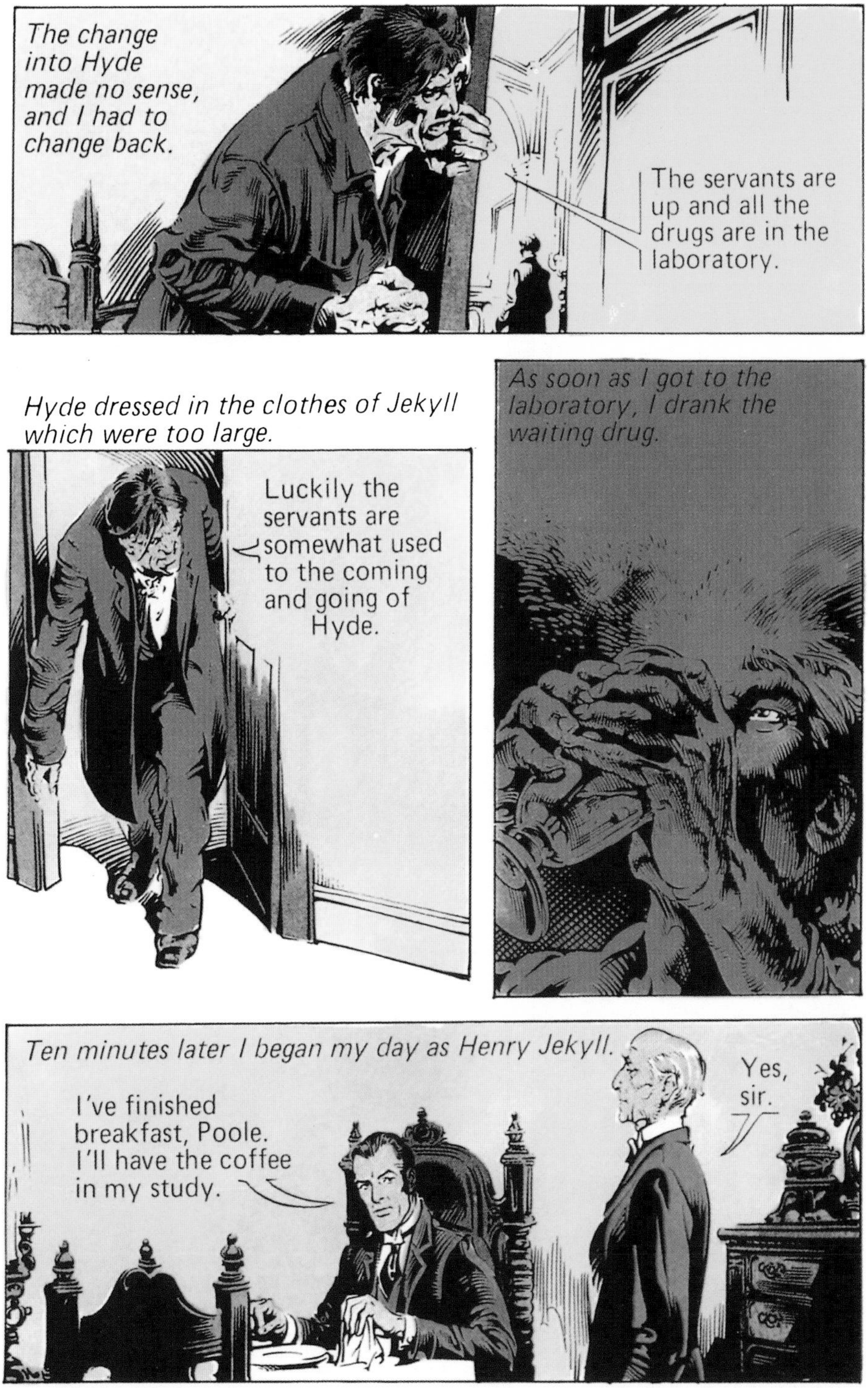
The change into Hyde made no sense, and I had to change back.
The servants are up and all the drugs are in the laboratory.
Hyde dressed in the clothes of Jekyll which were too large.
Luckily the servants are somewhat used to the coming and going of Hyde.
As soon as I got to the laboratory, I drank the waiting drug.
Ten minutes later I began my day as Henry Jekyll.
I've finished breakfast, Poole. I'll have the coffee in my study.
Yes, sir.

Changing into Hyde without drinking the magic drug seemed to spell out my future fate. . .Death!

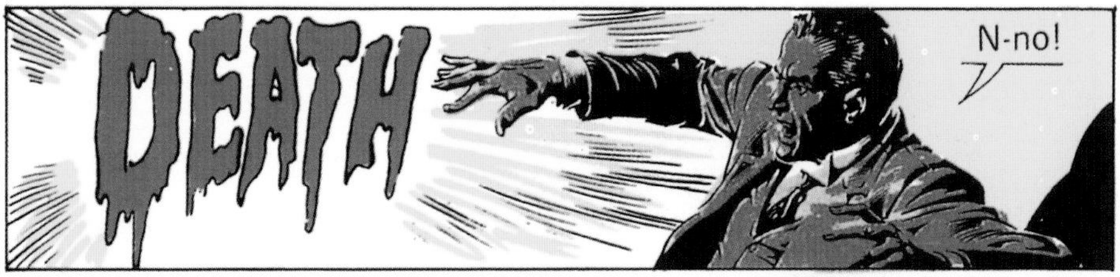
DEATH
N-no!

I thought a lot about my double life.

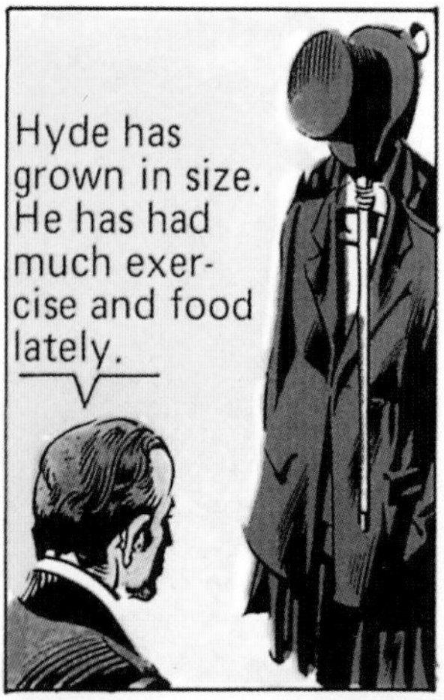
Hyde has grown in size. He has had much exercise and food lately.

I was worried that I might become Hyde forever—not be able to change back.

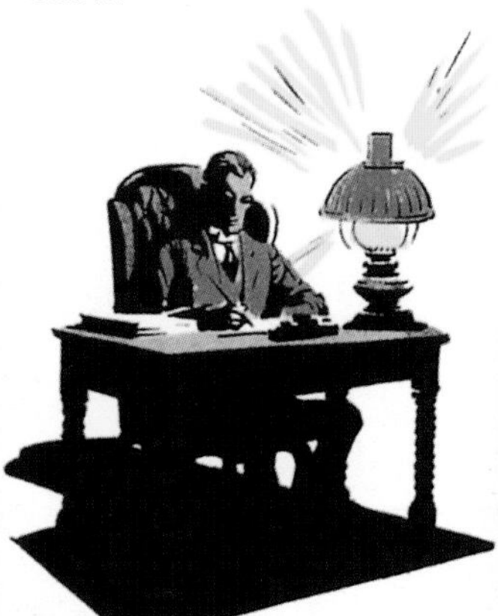

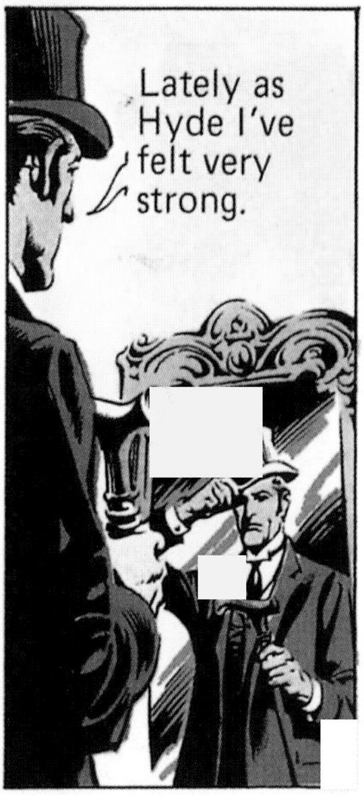
Lately as Hyde I've felt very strong.

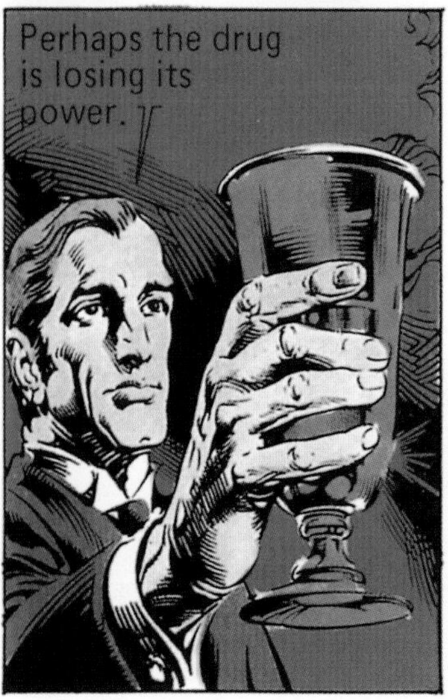
Perhaps the drug is losing its power.

Changing into Hyde had been hard at first. Now it became easier and easier.

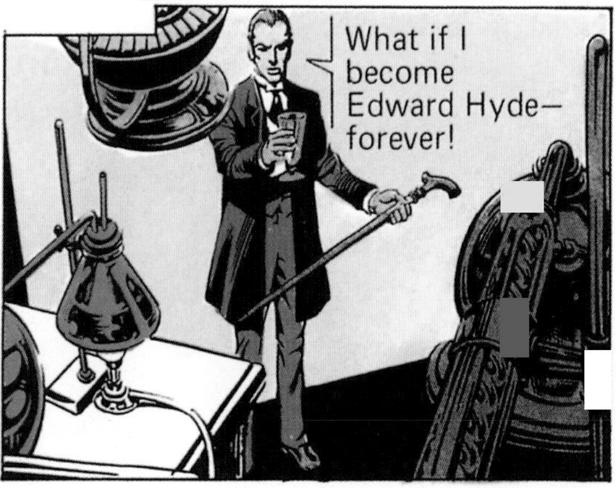
What if I become Edward Hyde—forever!

I knew I had to choose between the two. . .Jekyll helped plan and enjoyed the things Hyde did. . .but Hyde wanted to know nothing of Jekyll.

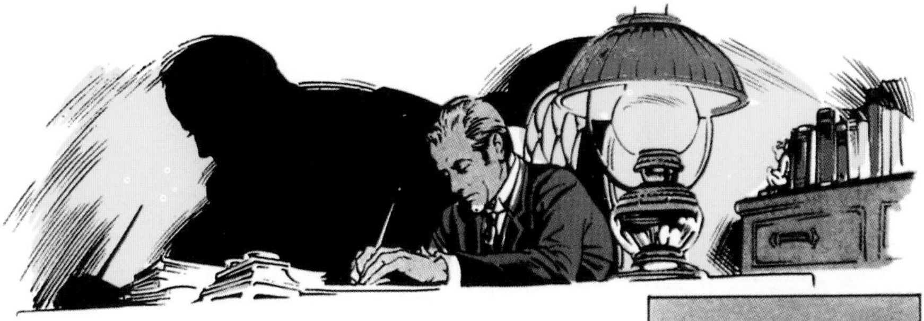

To always remain as Jekyll would mean giving up the fun that I now openly enjoyed as Hyde.

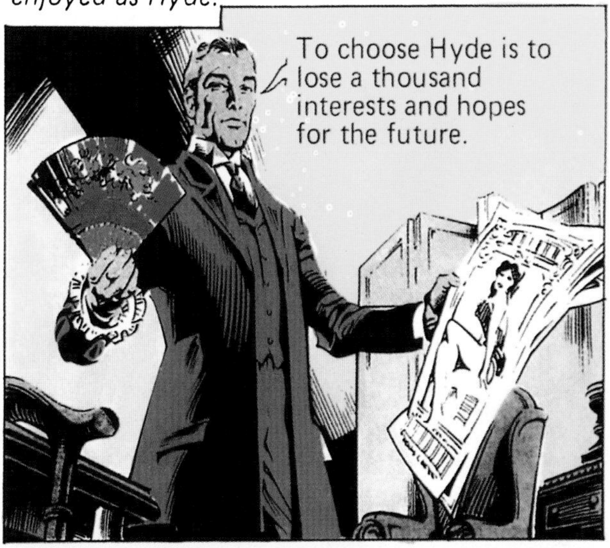
To choose Hyde is to lose a thousand interests and hopes for the future.

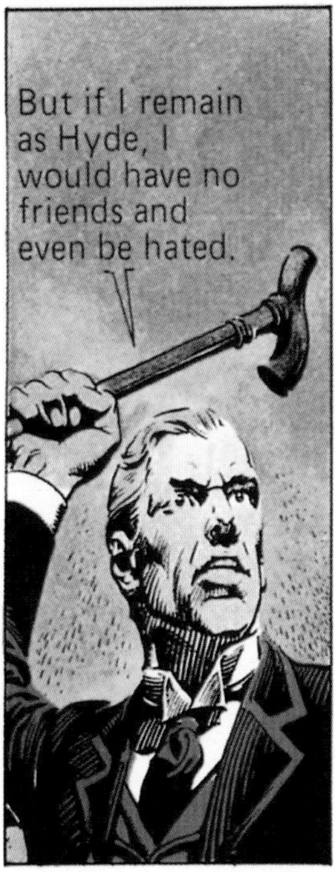
But if I remain as Hyde, I would have no friends and even be hated.

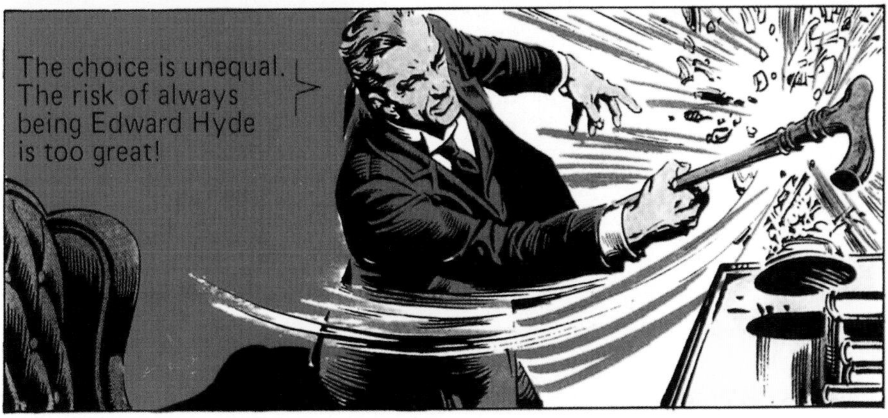
The choice is unequal. The risk of always being Edward Hyde is too great!

I chose Jekyll the better part of me and for two months I was true to my choice.

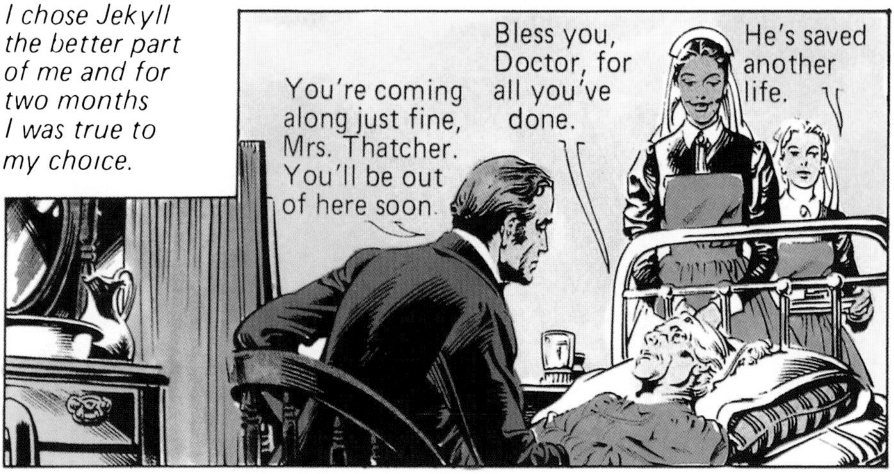
You're coming along just fine, Mrs. Thatcher. You'll be out of here soon.
Bless you, Doctor, for all you've done.
He's saved another life.

I worked harder at being a good doctor than ever before.

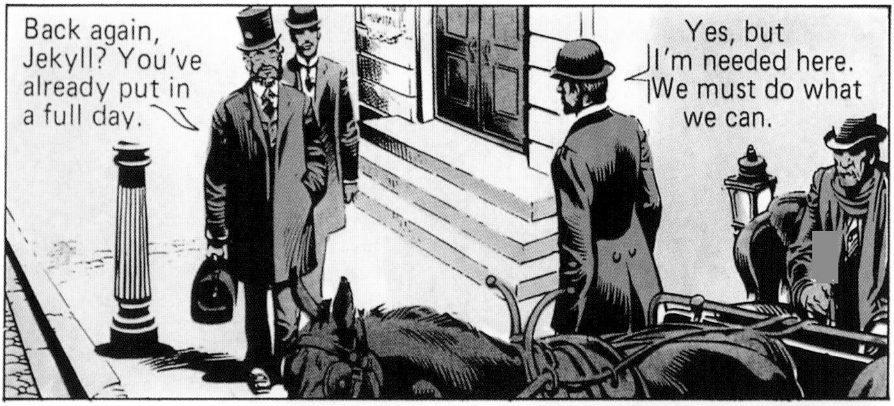
Back again, Jekyll? You've already put in a full day.
Yes, but I'm needed here. We must do what we can.

But time began at last to take away fears. The joy of hard work faded. The Hyde in me longed to be free.

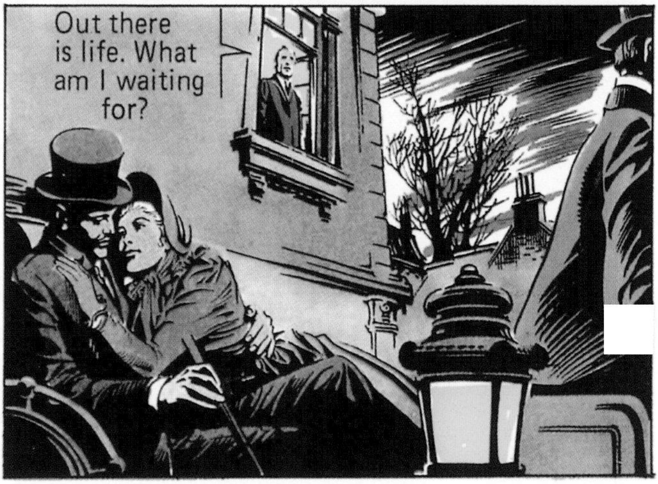
Out there is life. What am I waiting for?

At last, in an hour of weakness, I once again mixed and swallowed the drug.

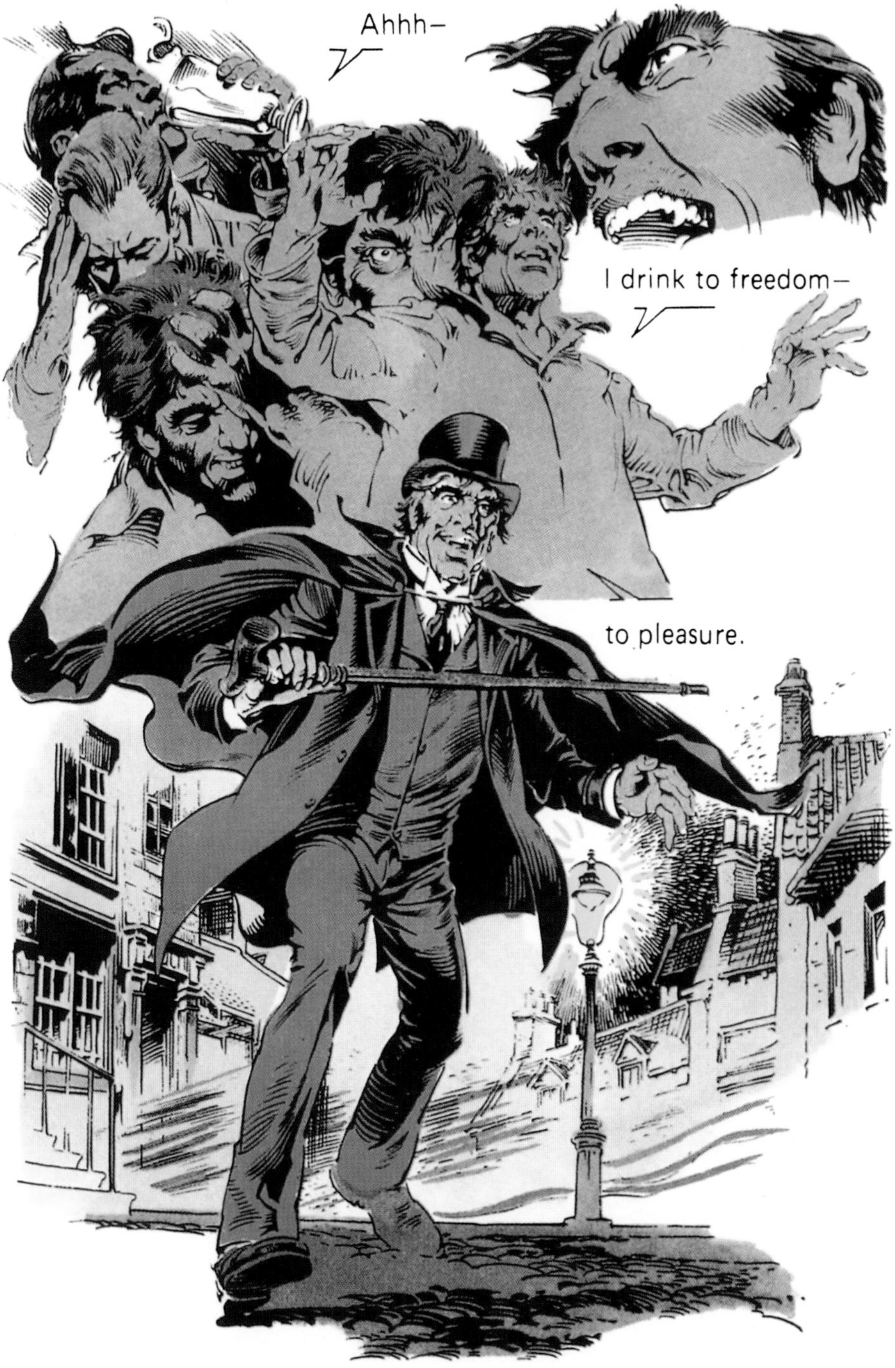
Ahhh–
I drink to freedom–
to pleasure.

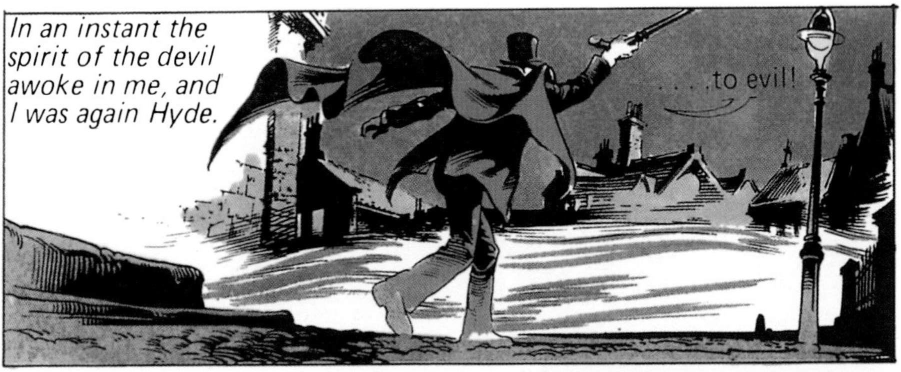
In an instant the spirit of the devil awoke in me, and I was again Hyde.
. . . .to evil!

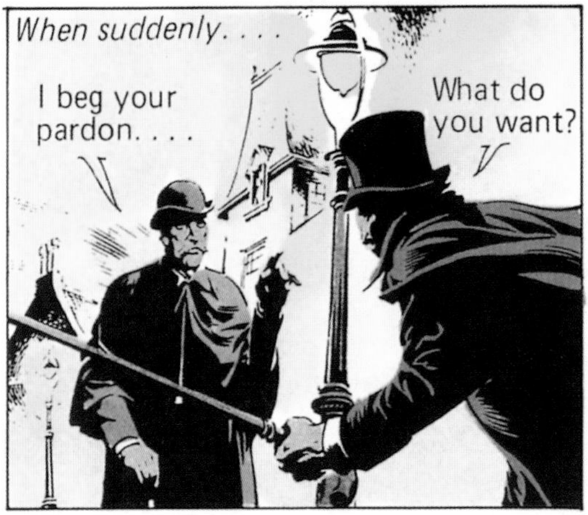
When suddenly. . . .
I beg your pardon. . . .
What do you want?

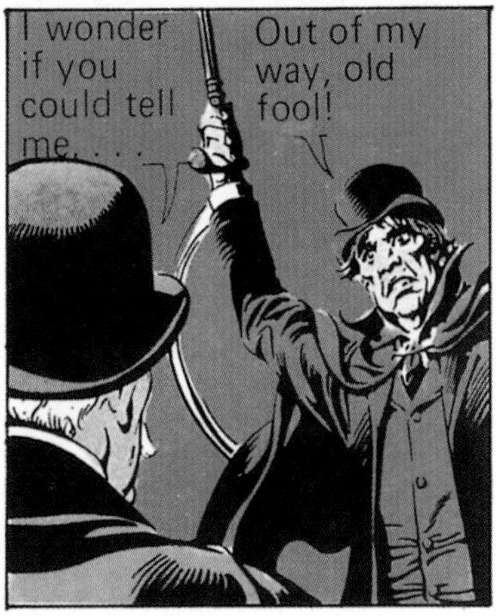
I wonder if you could tell me. . . .
Out of my way, old fool!

The devil in me had been shut up too long. It came roaring out.

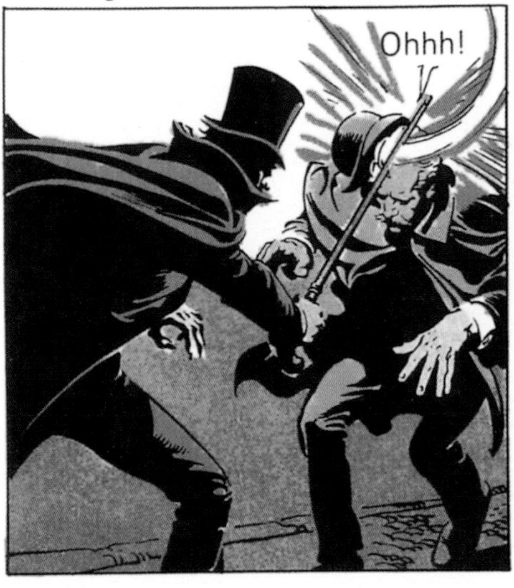
Ohhh!

I beat the old man, enjoying every blow.

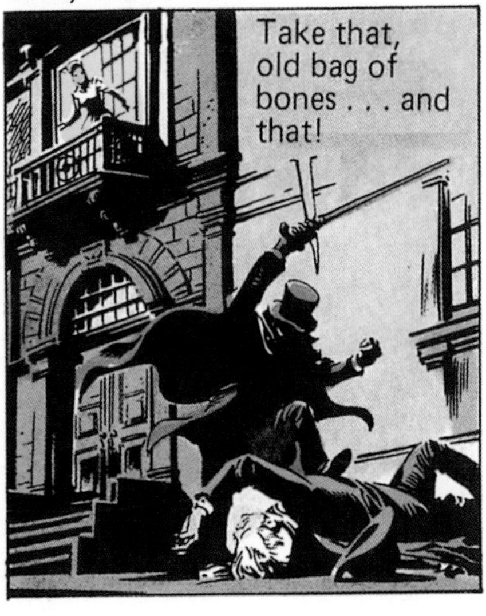
Take that, old bag of bones . . . and that!

Meanwhile, from across the road, a maid watched what happened. . . .

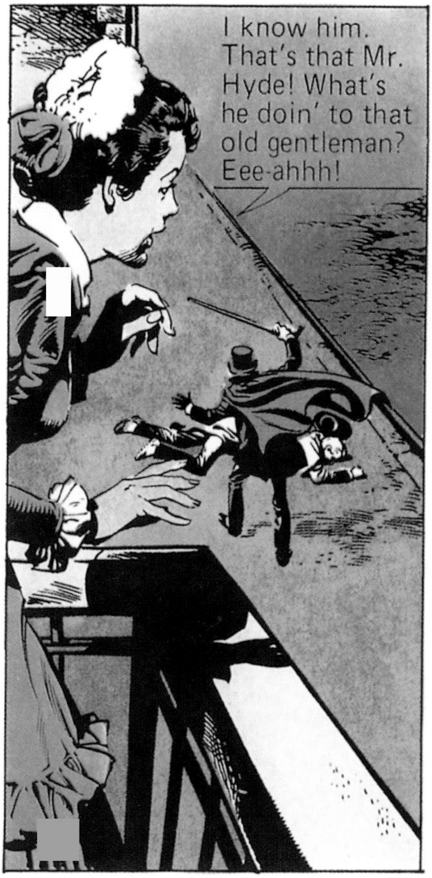
I know him. That's that Mr. Hyde! What's he doin' to that old gentleman? Eee-ahhh!

Suddenly, in my madness, cold terror filled my heart.

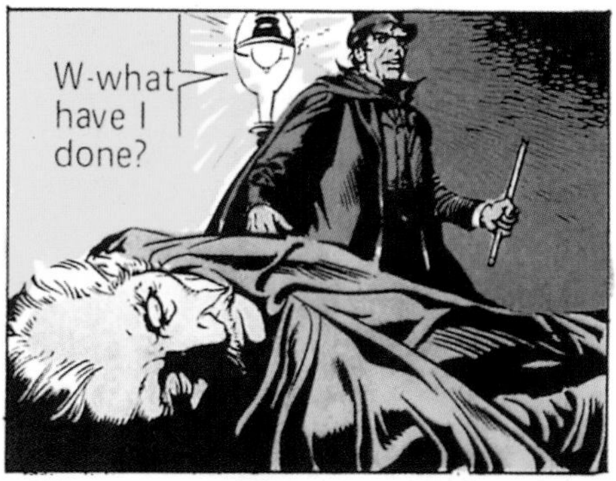
W-what have I done?

Shaking with fear, but glad at what I had done, I turned and ran.

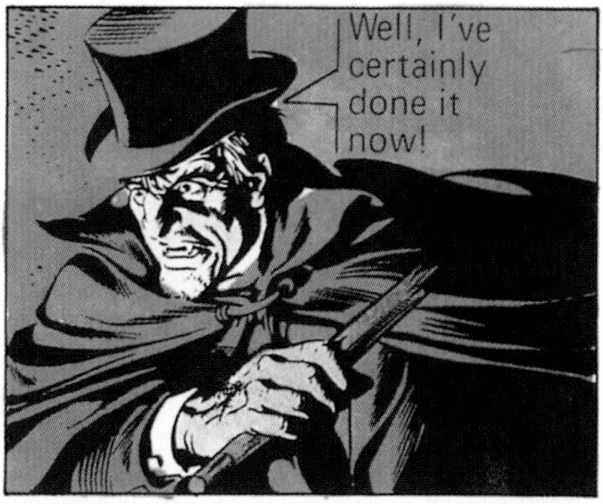
Well, I've certainly done it now!

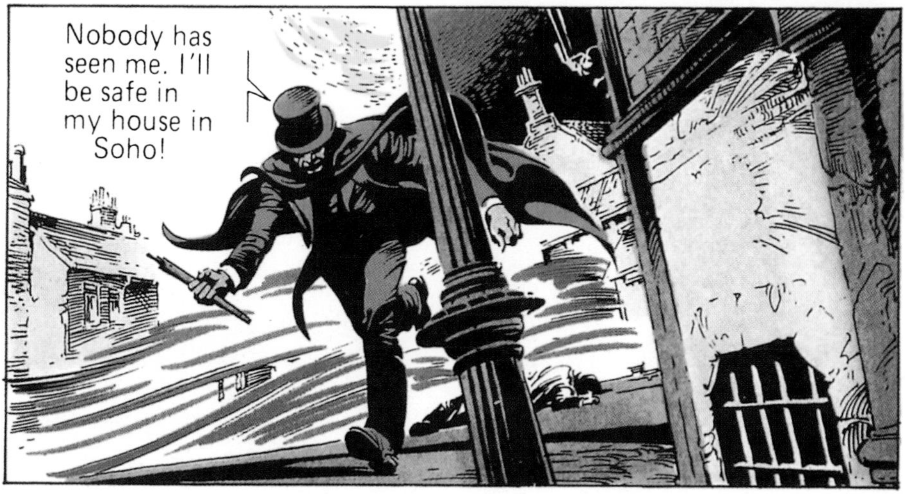
Nobody has seen me. I'll be safe in my house in Soho!

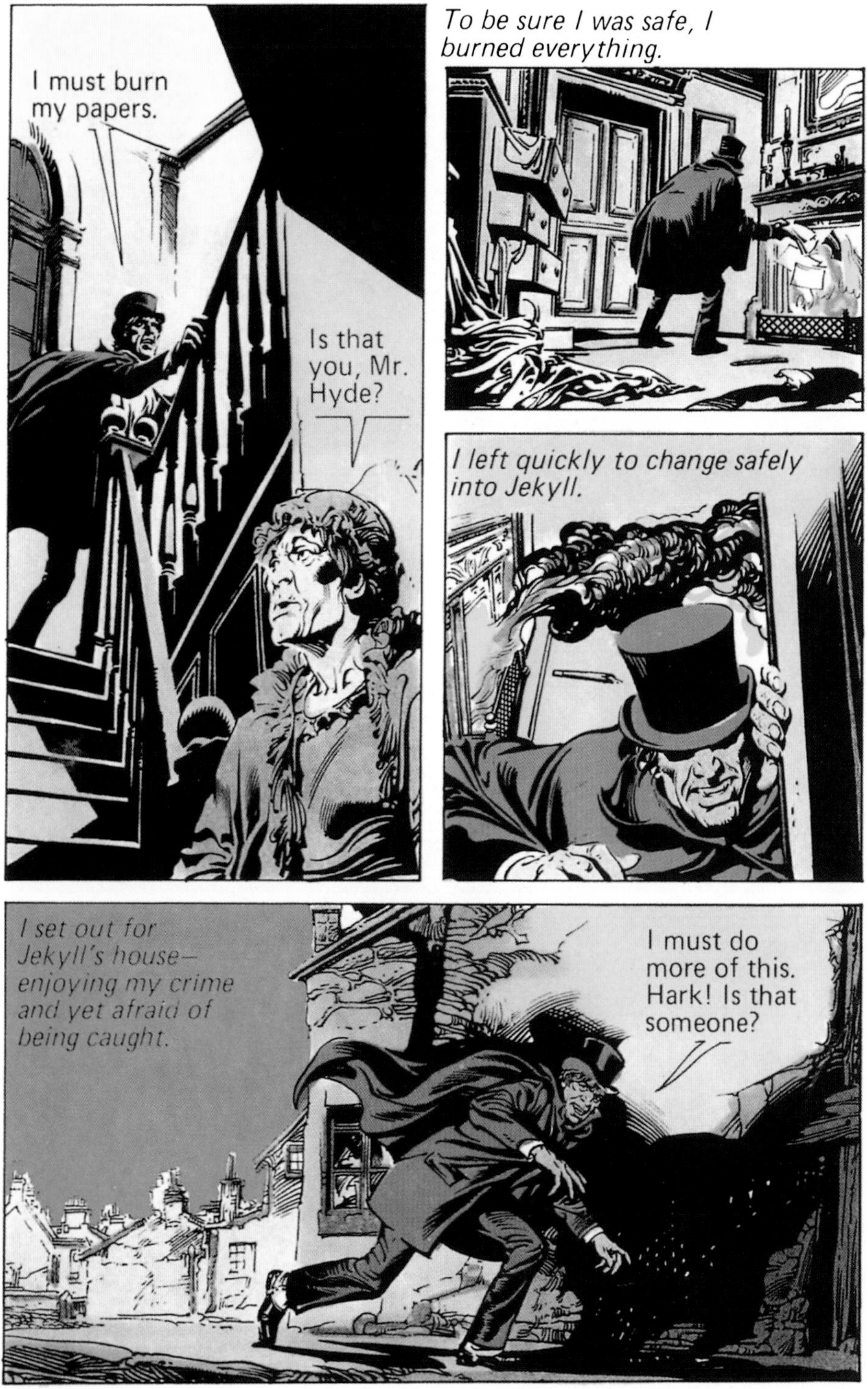
I must burn my papers.
Is that you, Mr. Hyde?
To be sure I was safe, I burned everything.
I left quickly to change safely into Jekyll.
I set out for Jekyll's house—enjoying my crime and yet afraid of being caught.
I must do more of this. Hark! Is that someone?

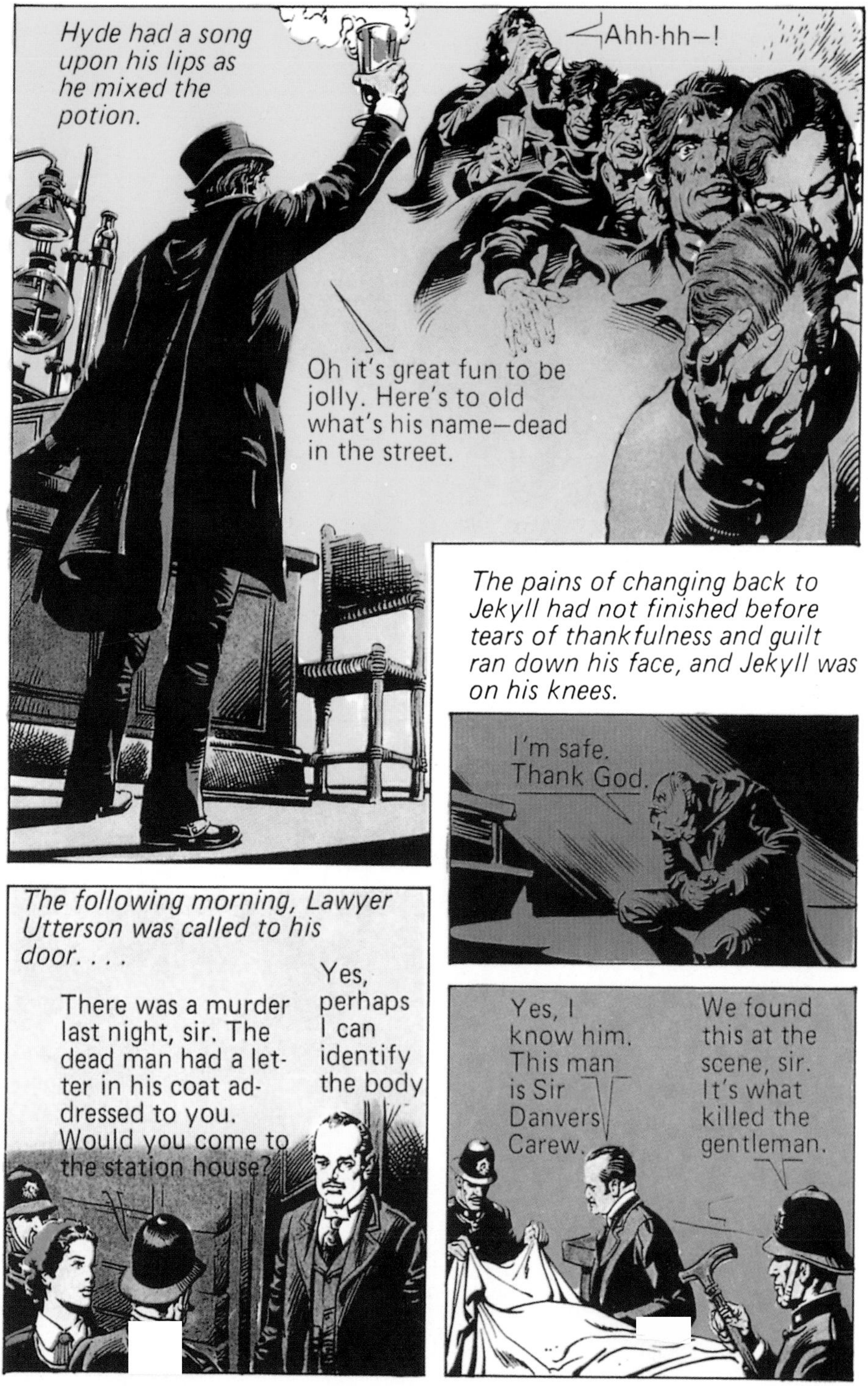
Hyde had a song upon his lips as he mixed the potion.
Ahh-hh–!
Oh it's great fun to be jolly. Here's to old what's his name—dead in the street.
The pains of changing back to Jekyll had not finished before tears of thankfulness and guilt ran down his face, and Jekyll was on his knees.
I'm safe. Thank God.
The following morning, Lawyer Utterson was called to his door. . . .
There was a murder last night, sir. The dead man had a letter in his coat addressed to you. Would you come to the station house?
Yes, perhaps I can identify the body
Yes, I know him. This man is Sir Danvers Carew.
We found this at the scene, sir. It's what killed the gentleman.

Utterson knew that the broken cane was one he had given Jekyll many years before.

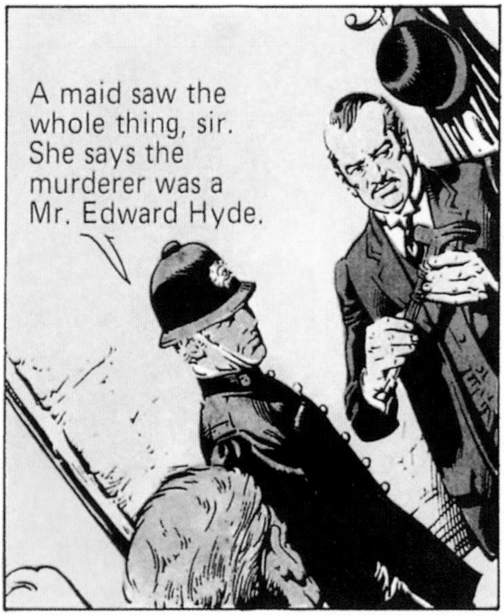
A maid saw the whole thing, sir. She says the murderer was a Mr. Edward Hyde.

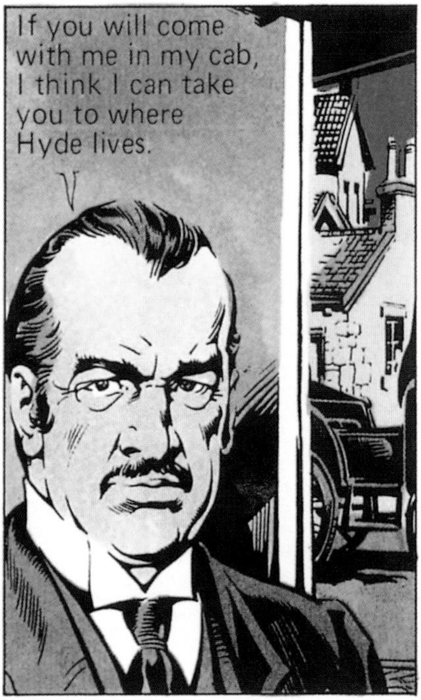
If you will come with me in my cab, I think I can take you to where Hyde lives.

Soon the cab arrived at Hyde's house in Soho.

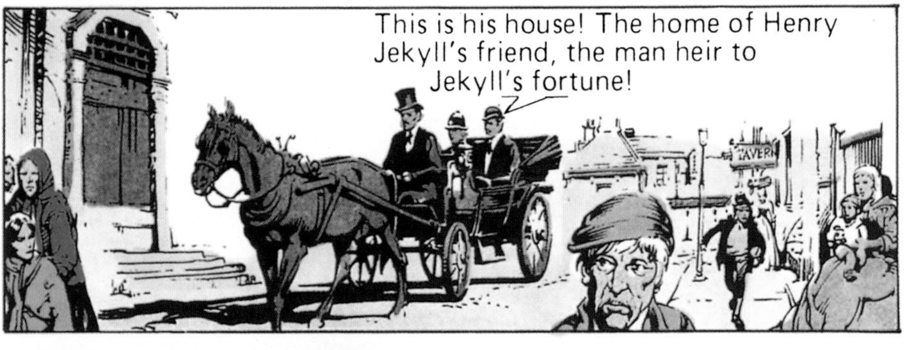
This is his house! The home of Henry Jekyll's friend, the man heir to Jekyll's fortune!
TAVERN

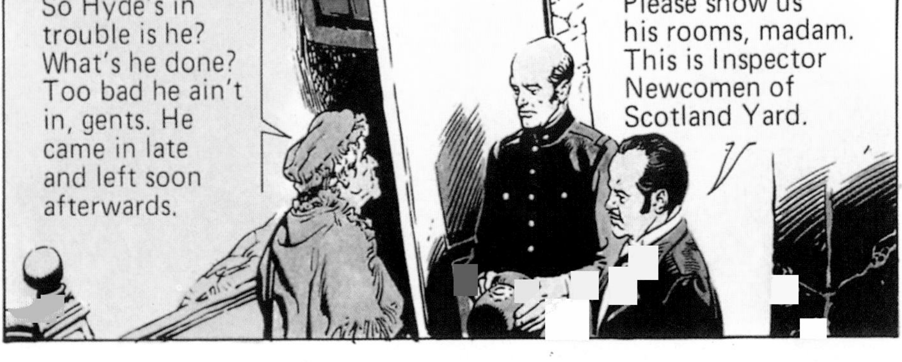
So Hyde's in trouble is he? What's he done? Too bad he ain't in, gents. He came in late and left soon afterwards.
Please show us his rooms, madam. This is Inspector Newcomen of Scotland Yard.

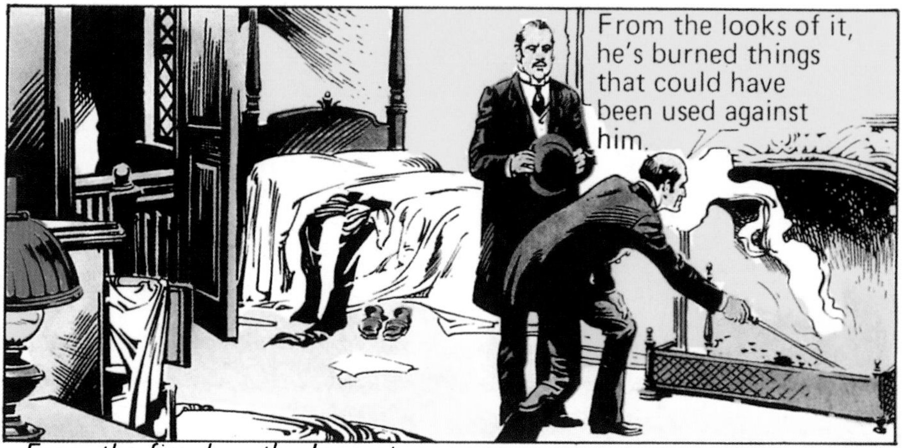
From the looks of it, he's burned things that could have been used against him.

From the fireplace the Inspector took some half burned papers.

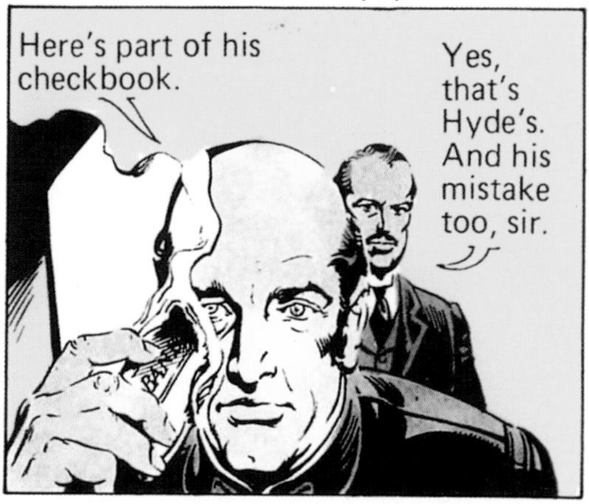
Here's part of his checkbook.
Yes, that's Hyde's. And his mistake too, sir.

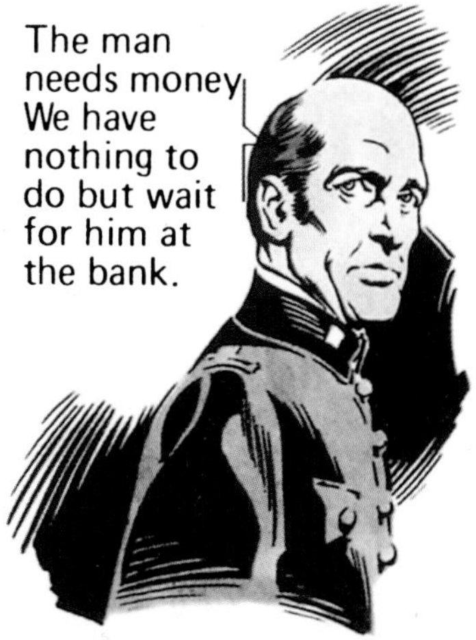
The man needs money We have nothing to do but wait for him at the bank.

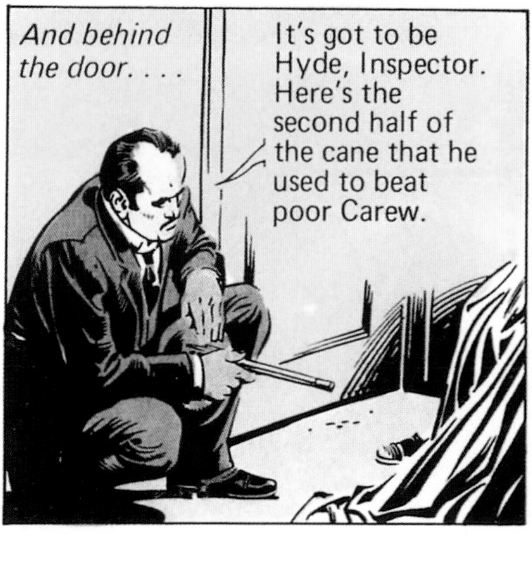
And behind the door. . . .
It's got to be Hyde, Inspector. Here's the second half of the cane that he used to beat poor Carew.

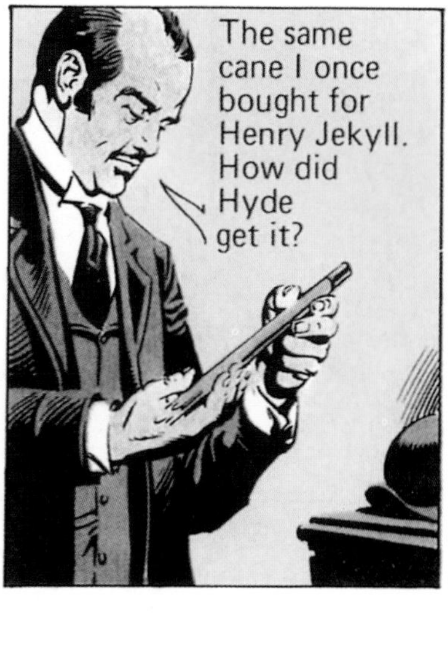
The same cane I once bought for Henry Jekyll. How did Hyde get it?

Later, Utterson went to the home of his friend, Jekyll. . . .

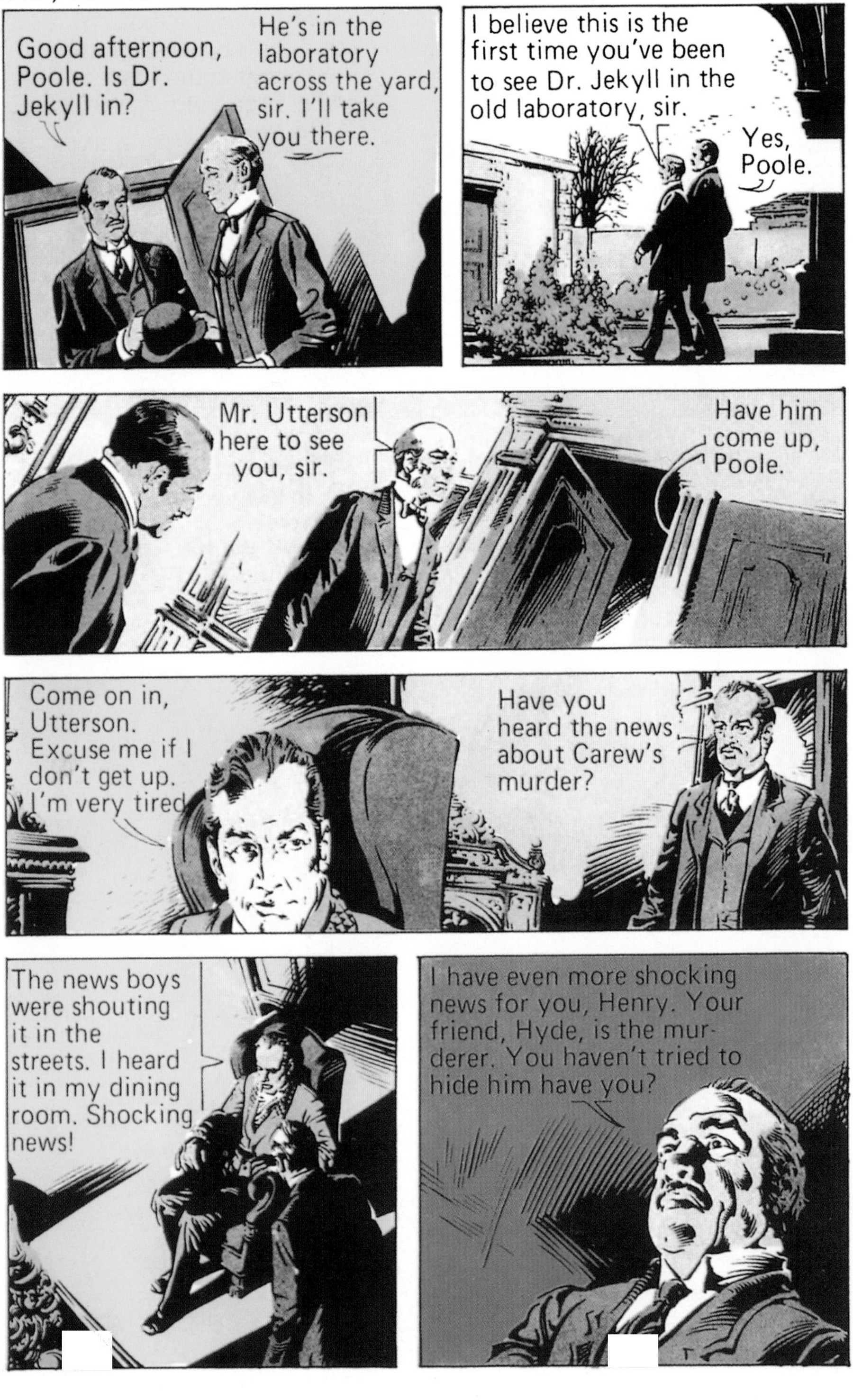
Good afternoon, Poole. Is Dr. Jekyll in?
He's in the laboratory across the yard, sir. I'll take you there.
I believe this is the first time you've been to see Dr. Jekyll in the old laboratory, sir.
Yes, Poole.
Mr. Utterson here to see you, sir.
Have him come up, Poole.
Come on in, Utterson. Excuse me if I don't get up. I'm very tired.
Have you heard the news about Carew's murder?
The news boys were shouting it in the streets. I heard it in my dining room. Shocking news!
I have even more shocking news for you, Henry. Your friend, Hyde, is the murderer. You haven't tried to hide him have you?

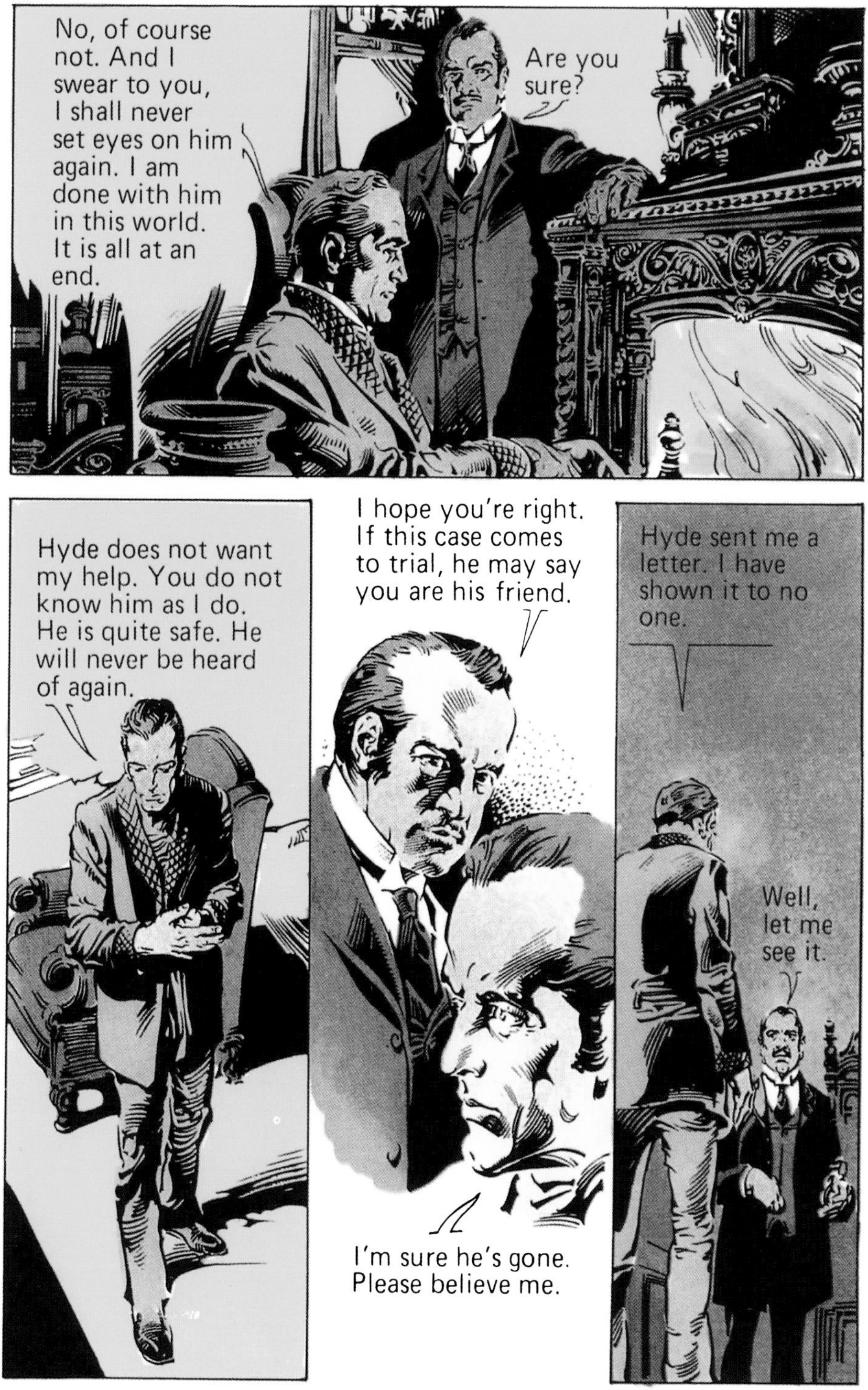
No, of course not. And I swear to you, I shall never set eyes on him again. I am done with him in this world. It is all at an end.
Are you sure?
Hyde does not want my help. You do not know him as I do. He is quite safe. He will never be heard of again.
I hope you're right. If this case comes to trial, he may say you are his friend.
I'm sure he's gone. Please believe me.
Hyde sent me a letter. I have shown it to no one.
Well, let me see it.

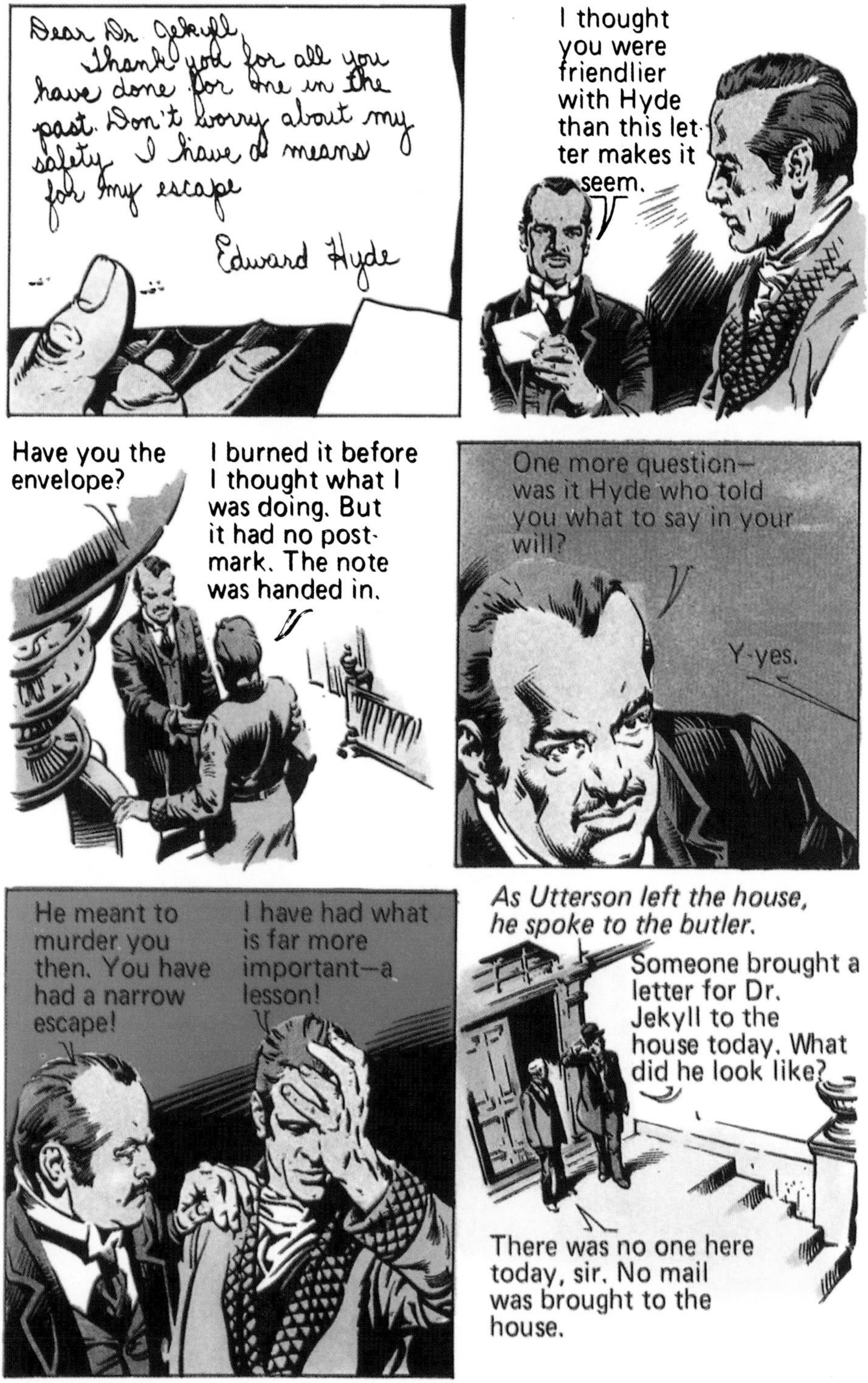
Dear Dr. Jekyll
Thank you for all you have done for me in the past. Don't worry about my safety. I have a means for my escape
Edward Hyde
I thought you were friendlier with Hyde than this letter makes it seem.
Have you the envelope?
I burned it before I thought what I was doing. But it had no postmark. The note was handed in.
One more question—was it Hyde who told you what to say in your will?
Y-yes.
He meant to murder you then. You have had a narrow escape!
I have had what is far more important—a lesson!
As Utterson left the house, he spoke to the butler.
Someone brought a letter for Dr. Jekyll to the house today. What did he look like?
There was no one here today, sir. No mail was brought to the house.

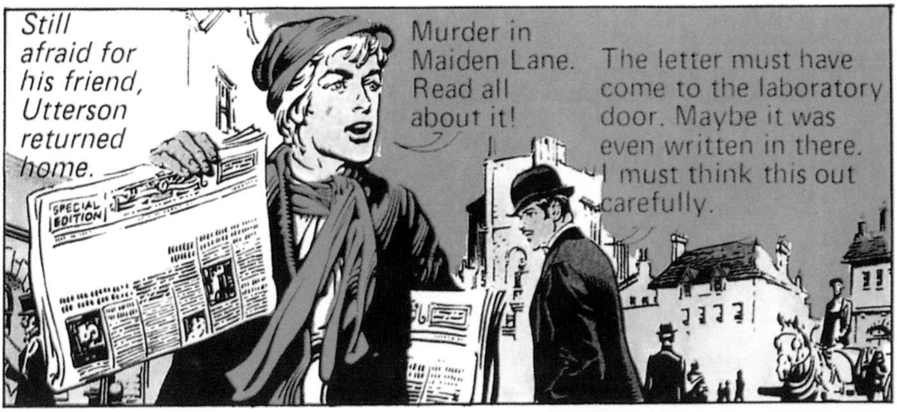
Still afraid for his friend, Utterson returned home.
SPECIAL EDITION
Murder in Maiden Lane. Read all about it!
The letter must have come to the laboratory door. Maybe it was even written in there. I must think this out carefully.

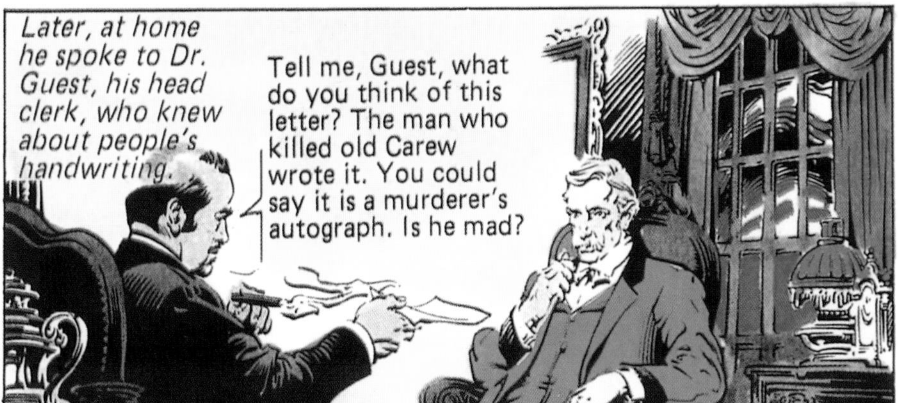
Later, at home he spoke to Dr. Guest, his head clerk, who knew about people's handwriting.
Tell me, Guest, what do you think of this letter? The man who killed old Carew wrote it. You could say it is a murderer's autograph. Is he mad?

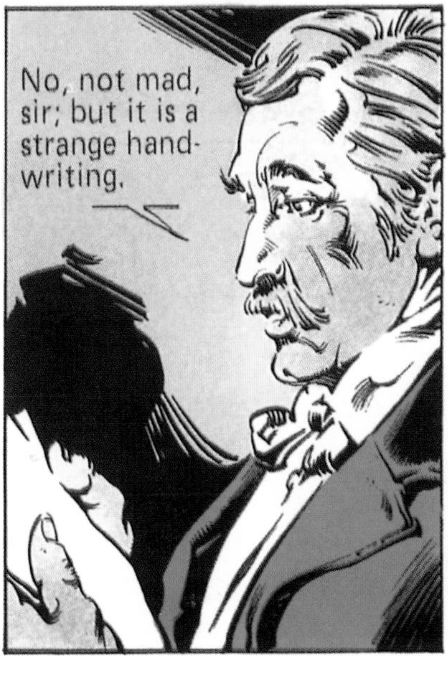
No, not mad, sir; but it is a strange handwriting.

At that moment the butler delivered a message.

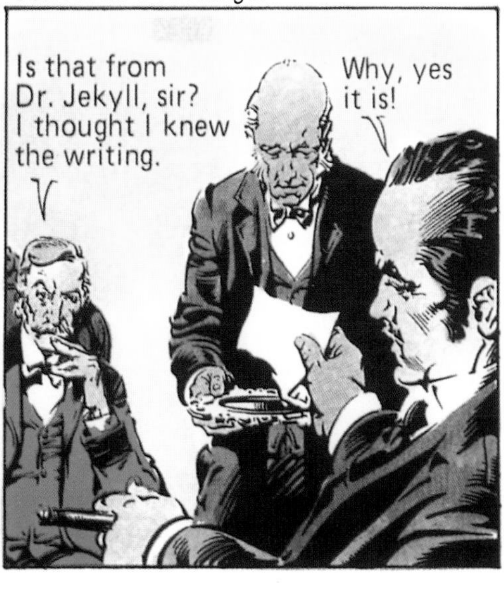
Is that from Dr. Jekyll, sir? I thought I knew the writing.
Why, yes it is!

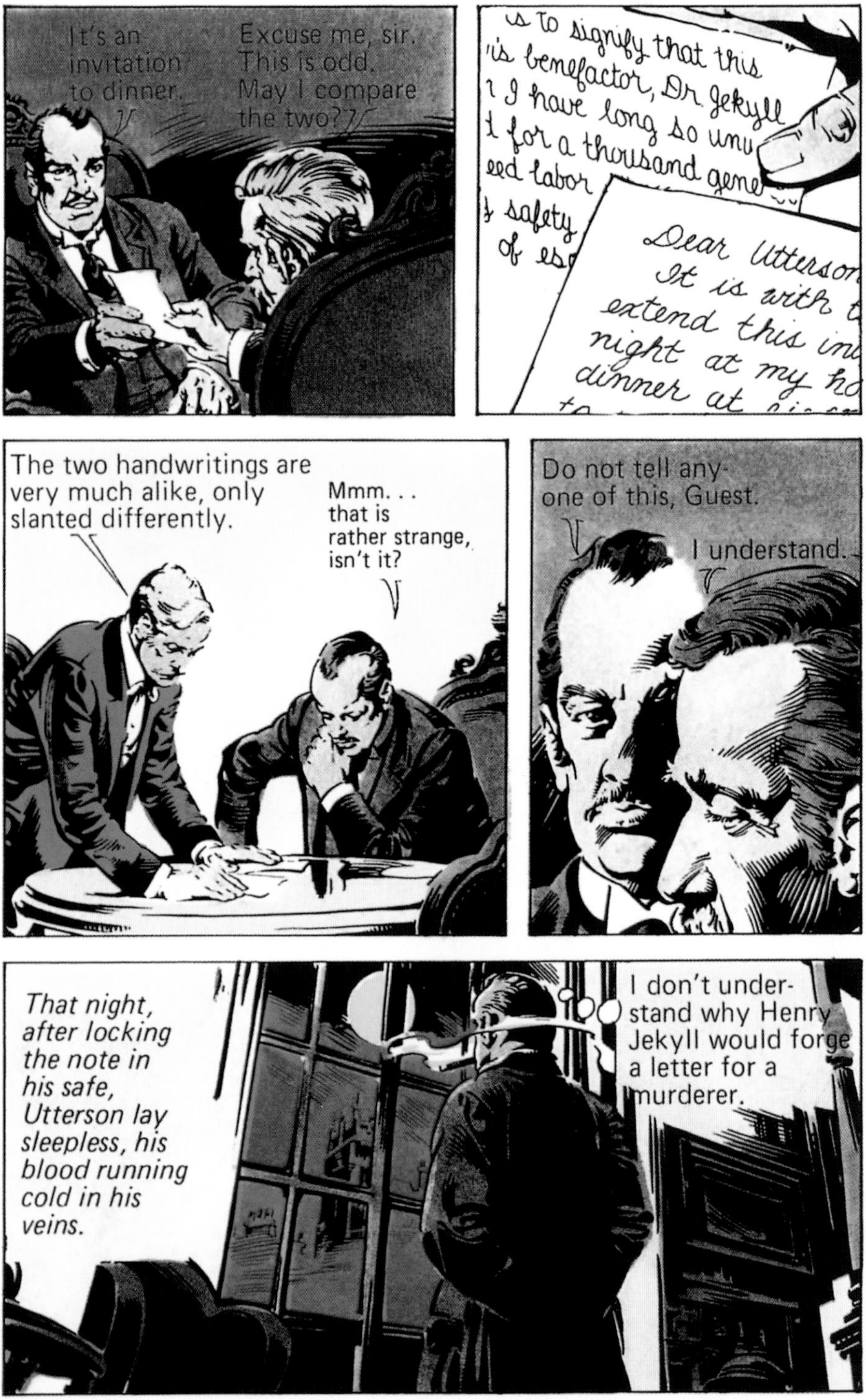
It's an invitation to dinner.
Excuse me, sir. This is odd. May I compare the two?
to signify that this
benefactor, Dr. Jekyll
I have long so
for a thousand
labor
safety
Dear Utterson
It is with
extend this
night at my
dinner at
The two handwritings are very much alike, only slanted differently.
Mmm. . . that is rather strange, isn't it?
Do not tell any-one of this, Guest.
I understand.
That night, after locking the note in his safe, Utterson lay sleepless, his blood running cold in his veins.
I don't under-stand why Henry Jekyll would forge a letter for a murderer.

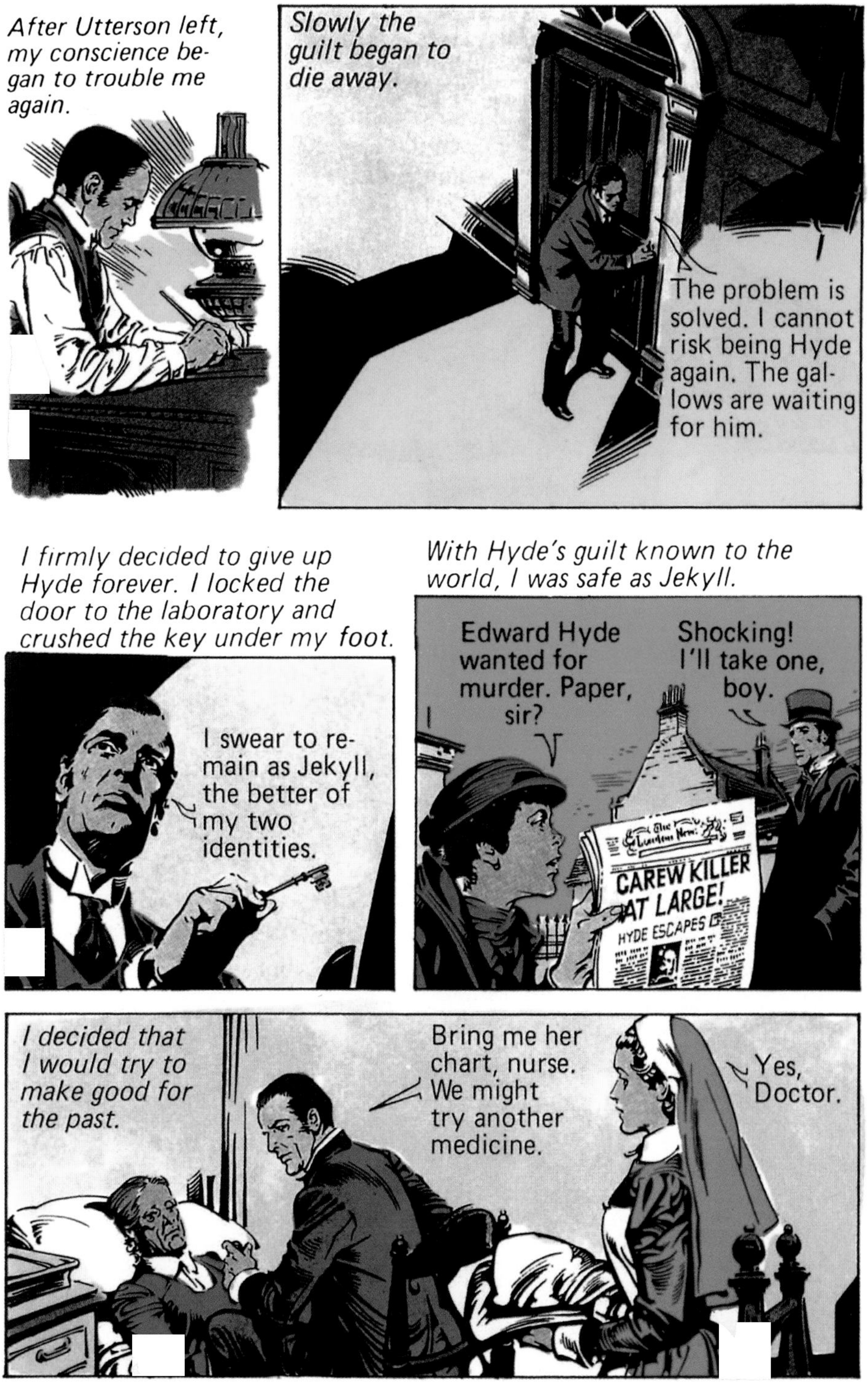
After Utterson left, my conscience began to trouble me again.
Slowly the guilt began to die away.
The problem is solved. I cannot risk being Hyde again. The gallows are waiting for him.
I firmly decided to give up Hyde forever. I locked the door to the laboratory and crushed the key under my foot.
I swear to remain as Jekyll, the better of my two identities.
With Hyde's guilt known to the world, I was safe as Jekyll.
Edward Hyde wanted for murder. Paper, sir?
Shocking! I'll take one, boy.
CAREW KILLER AT LARGE!
HYDE ESCAPES
I decided that I would try to make good for the past.
Bring me her chart, nurse. We might try another medicine.
Yes, Doctor.

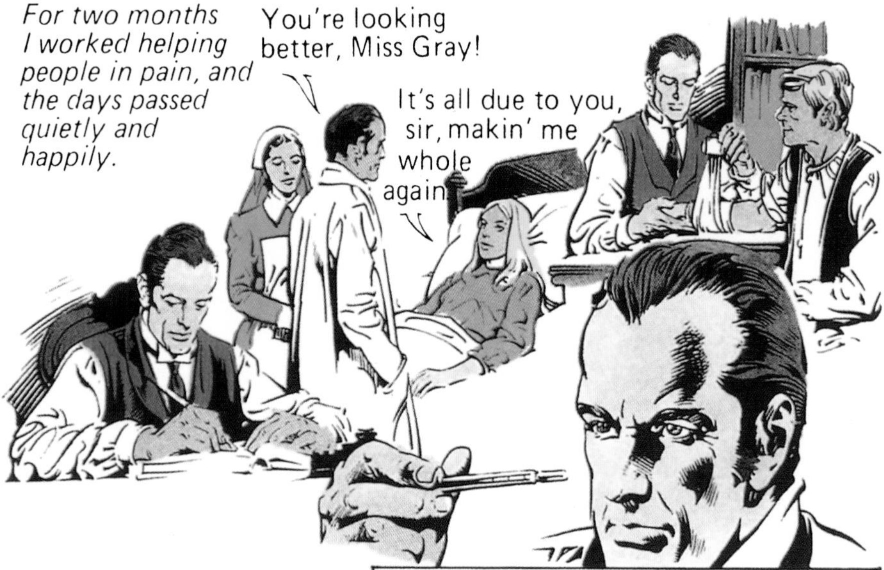
For two months I worked helping people in pain, and the days passed quietly and happily.
You're looking better, Miss Gray!
It's all due to you, sir, makin' me whole again.

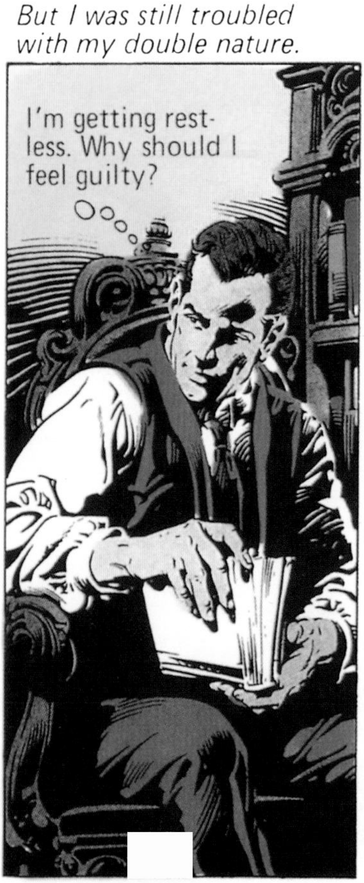
But I was still troubled with my double nature.
I'm getting restless. Why should I feel guilty?

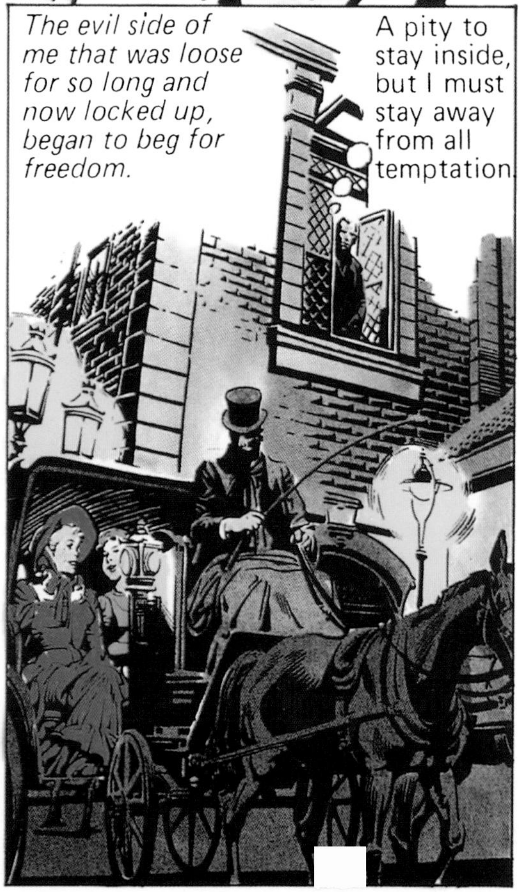
The evil side of me that was loose for so long and now locked up, began to beg for freedom.
A pity to stay inside, but I must stay away from all temptation.

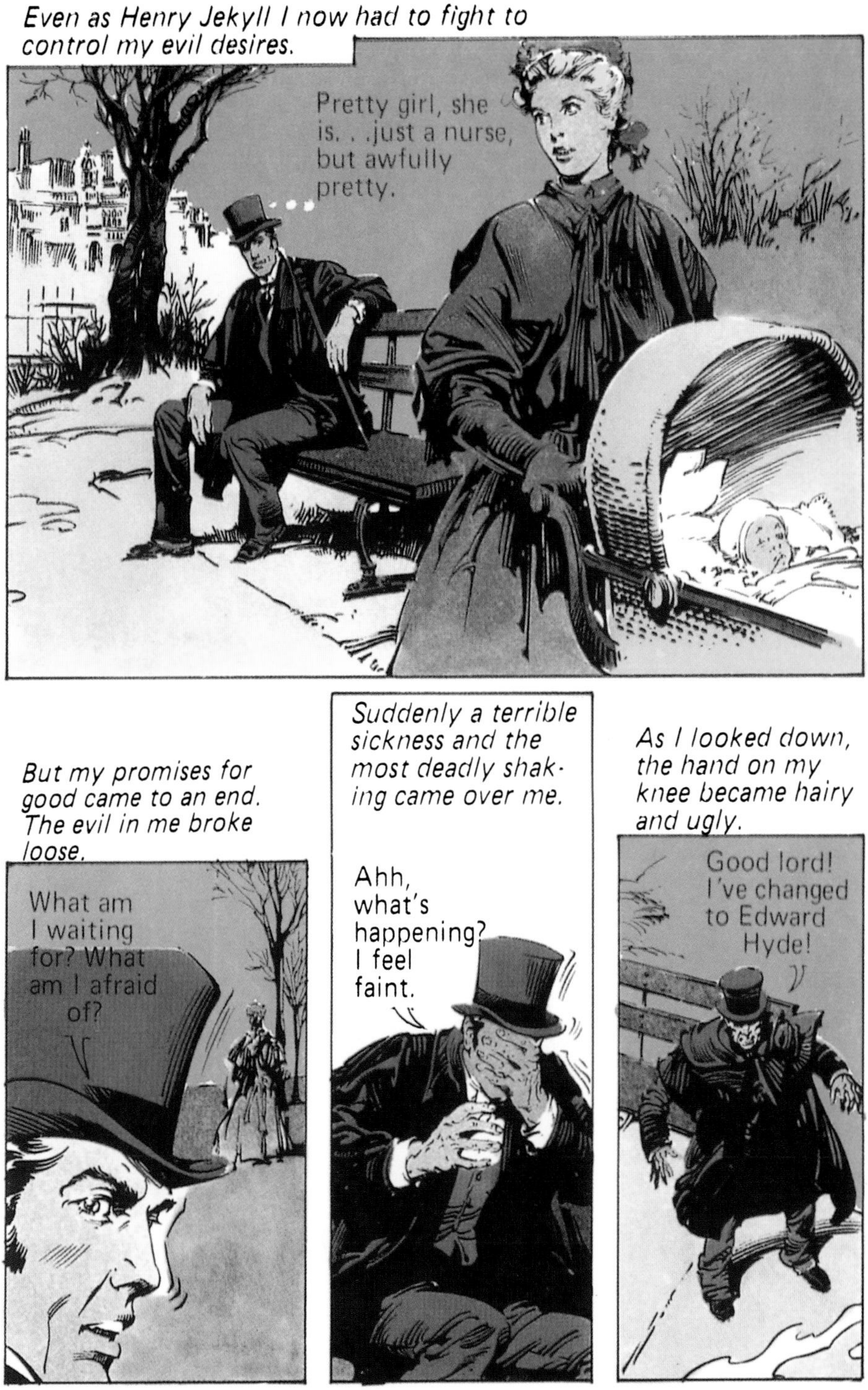
Even as Henry Jekyll I now had to fight to control my evil desires.
Pretty girl, she is. . .just a nurse, but awfully pretty.
But my promises for good came to an end. The evil in me broke loose.
What am I waiting for? What am I afraid of?
Suddenly a terrible sickness and the most deadly shak-ing came over me.
Ahh, what's happening? I feel faint.
As I looked down, the hand on my knee became hairy and ugly.
Good lord! I've changed to Edward Hyde!

A moment before I was a man respected by other men. Now I was Hyde—hunted, a known murderer headed for the gallows.

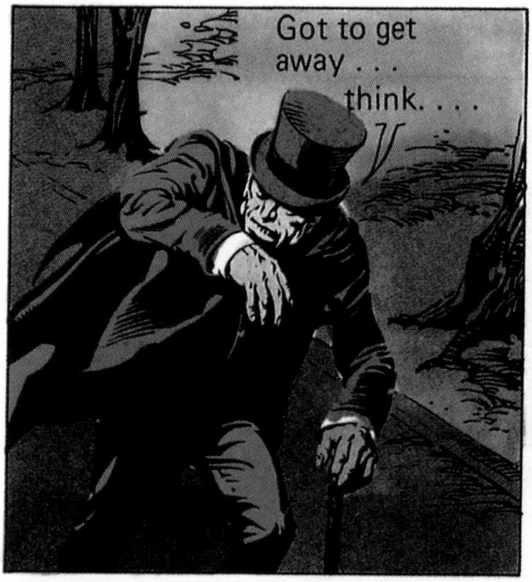
Got to get away . . . think. . . .

Jekyll would have gone to the police, but Hyde wished only to protect himself.

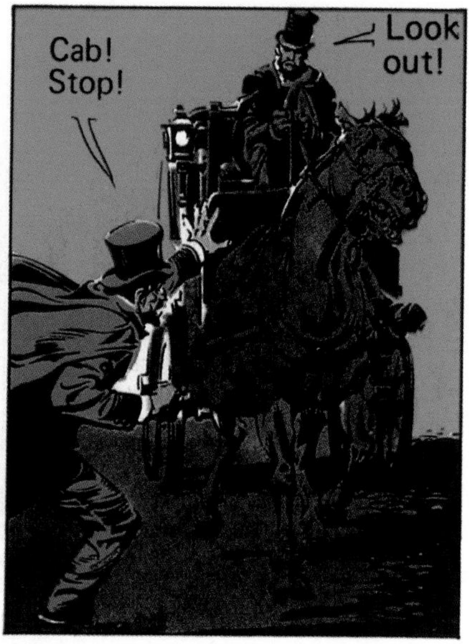
Cab! Stop!
Look out!

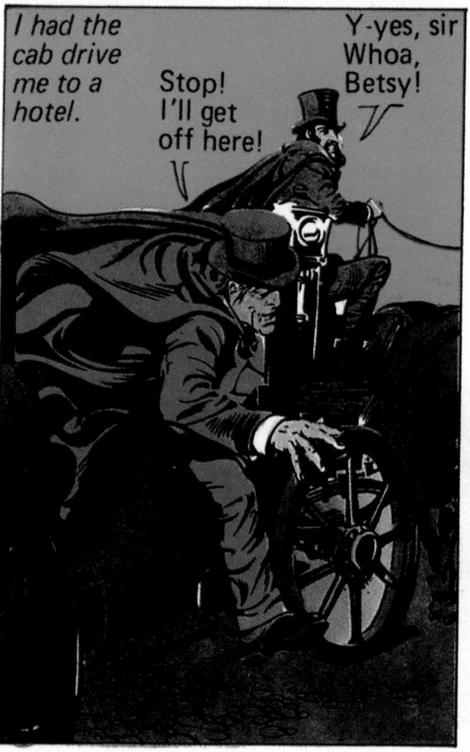
I had the cab drive me to a hotel.
Stop! I'll get off here!
Y-yes, sir
Whoa, Betsy!

When I was safe in a room, I wrote two letters—one to Dr. Lanyon and one to my butler, Poole.

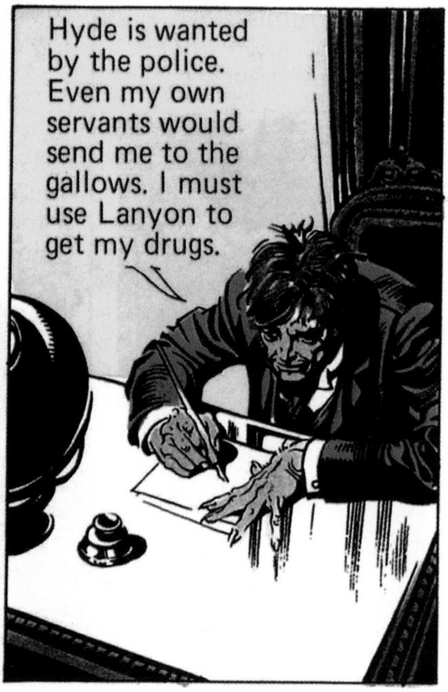
Hyde is wanted by the police. Even my own servants would send me to the gallows. I must use Lanyon to get my drugs.

And shortly afterward. . . .

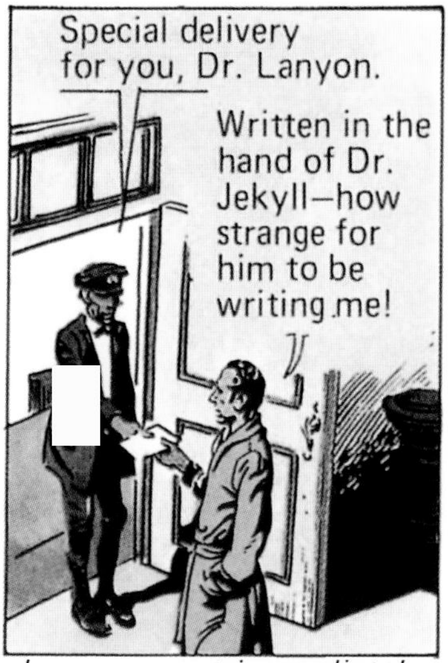
Special delivery for you, Dr. Lanyon.
Written in the hand of Dr. Jekyll—how strange for him to be writing me!

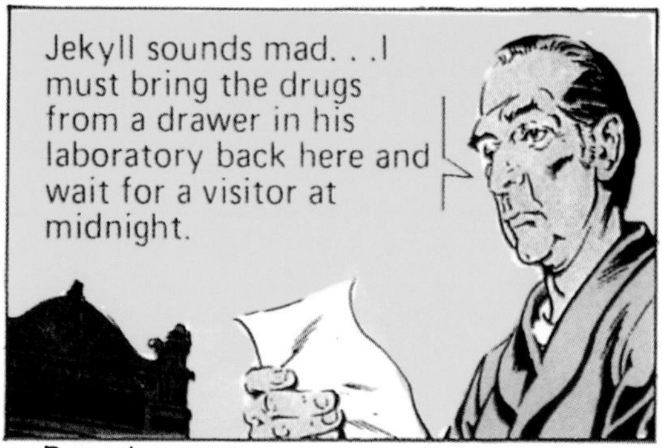
Jekyll sounds mad. . .I must bring the drugs from a drawer in his laboratory back here and wait for a visitor at midnight.

Dear Lanyon,

You are one of my oldest friends; and although we may have disagreed at times on scientific matters, I cannot remember any break in our friendship. My life, my reason, my honor are all at your mercy. . .if you fail me tonight.

Lanyon went immediately to Jekyll's house.

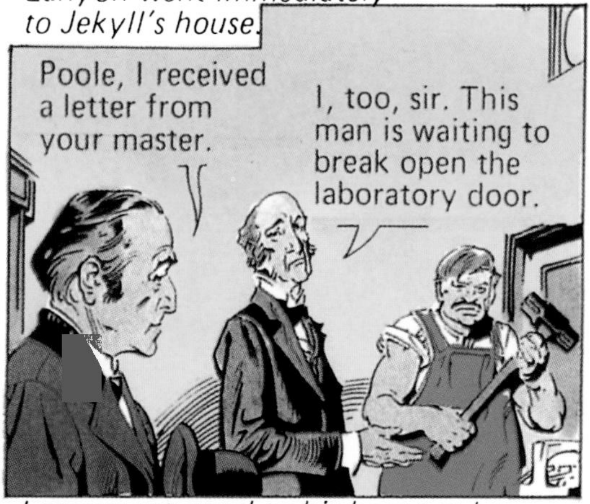
Poole, I received a letter from your master.
I, too, sir. This man is waiting to break open the laboratory door.

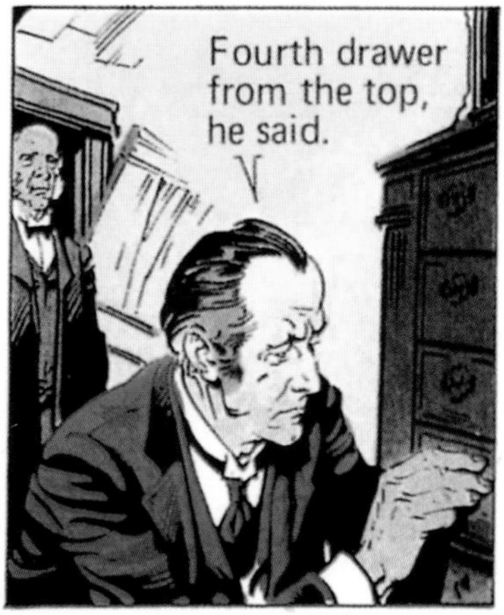
Fourth drawer from the top, he said.

Lanyon returned to his home as he had been told to do.

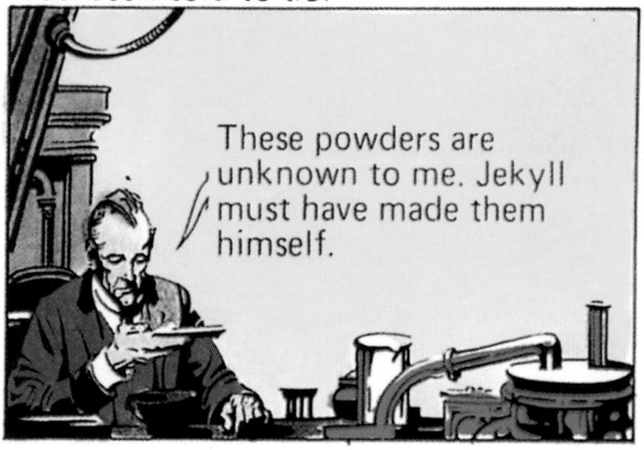
These powders are unknown to me. Jekyll must have made them himself.

Exactly at midnight. . . .

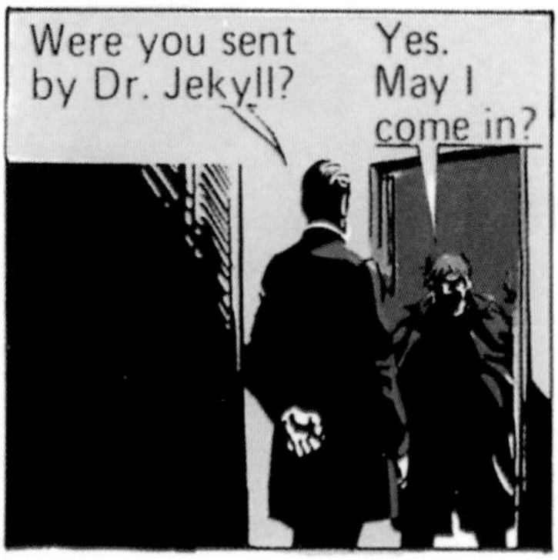
Were you sent by Dr. Jekyll?
Yes. May I come in?

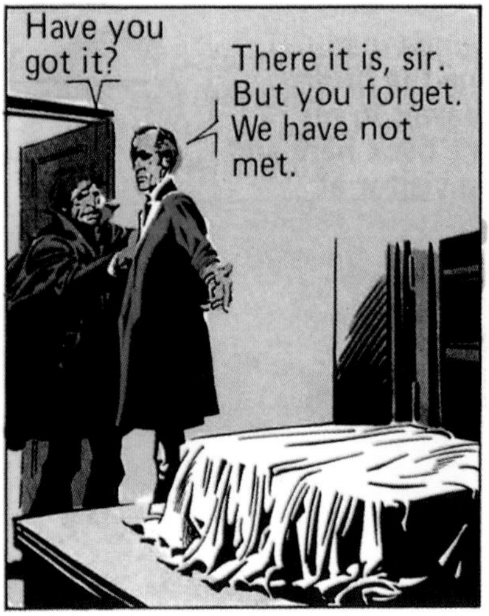
Have you got it?
There it is, sir. But you forget. We have not met.

At the sight of the drugs, Hyde gave out a sigh of relief.

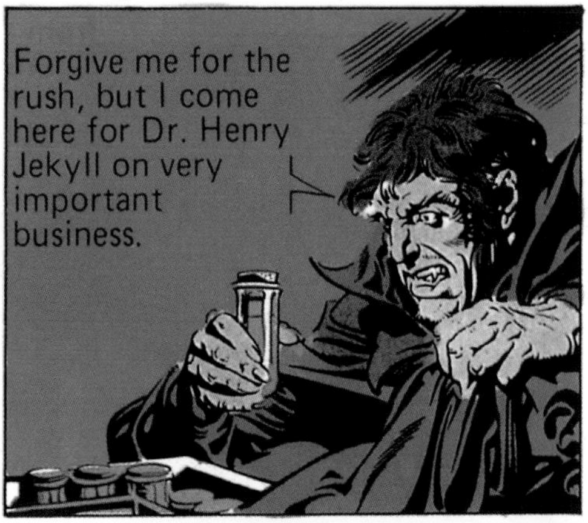
Forgive me for the rush, but I come here for Dr. Henry Jekyll on very important business.

Taking a glass, Lanyon's visitor quickly mixed the drugs.

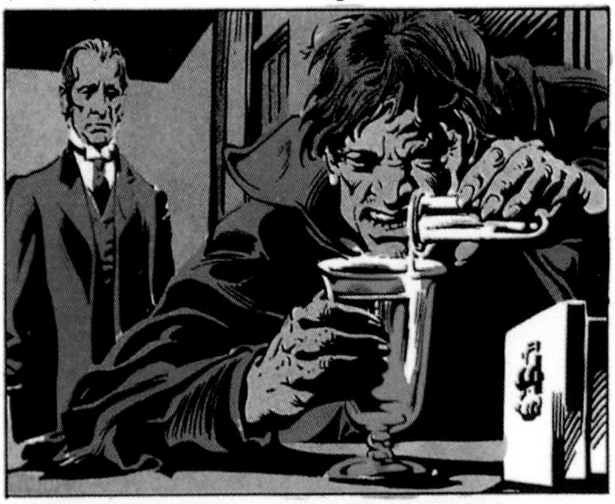

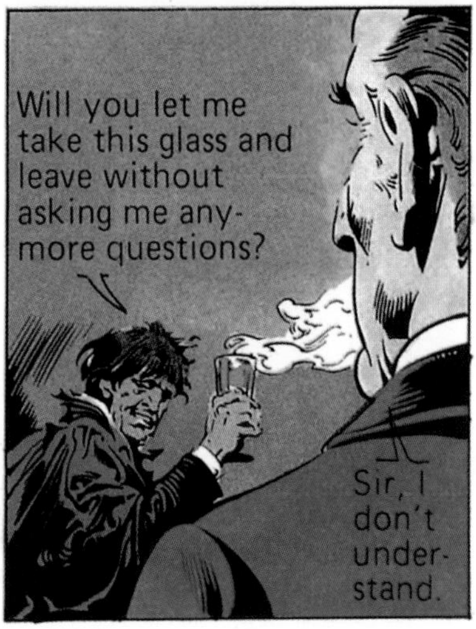
Will you let me take this glass and leave without asking me any-more questions?
Sir, I don't under-stand.

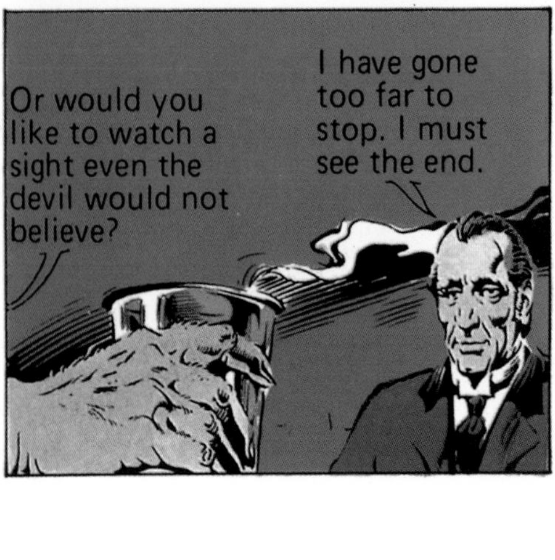
Or would you like to watch a sight even the devil would not believe?
I have gone too far to stop. I must see the end.

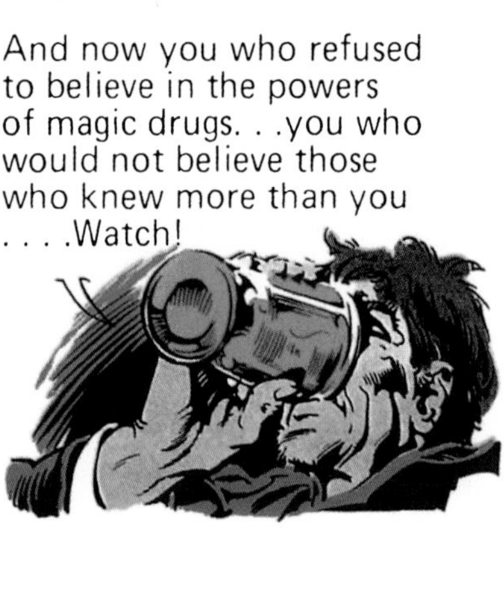
And now you who refused to believe in the powers of magic drugs. . .you who would not believe those who knew more than you . . . .Watch!

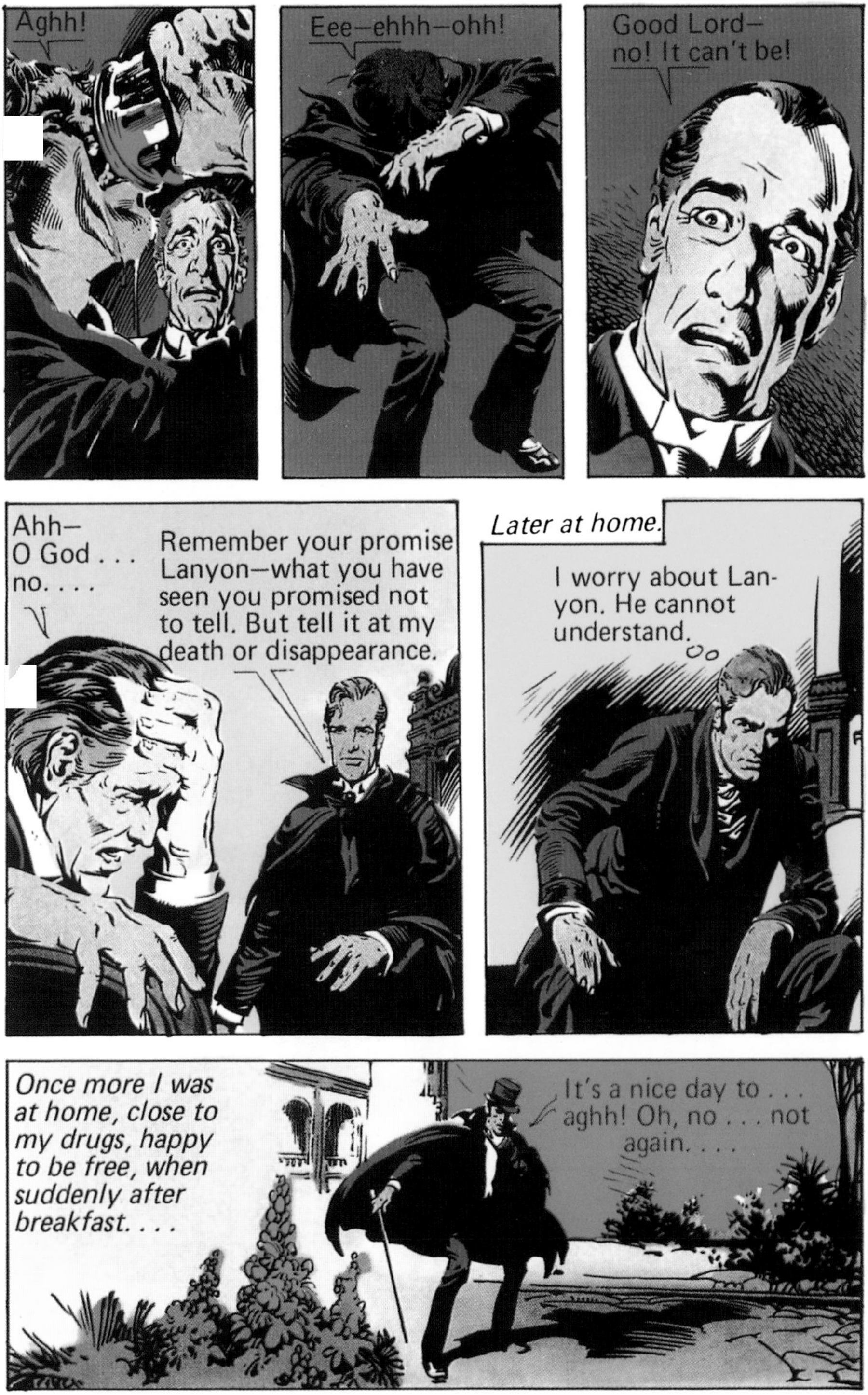
Aghh!
Eee–ehhh–ohh!
Good Lord– no! It can't be!
Ahh– O God . . . no. . . .
Remember your promise Lanyon–what you have seen you promised not to tell. But tell it at my death or disappearance.
Later at home.
I worry about Lanyon. He cannot understand.
Once more I was at home, close to my drugs, happy to be free, when suddenly after breakfast. . . .
It's a nice day to . . . aghh! Oh, no . . . not again. . . .

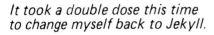

It took a double dose this time to change myself back to Jekyll.

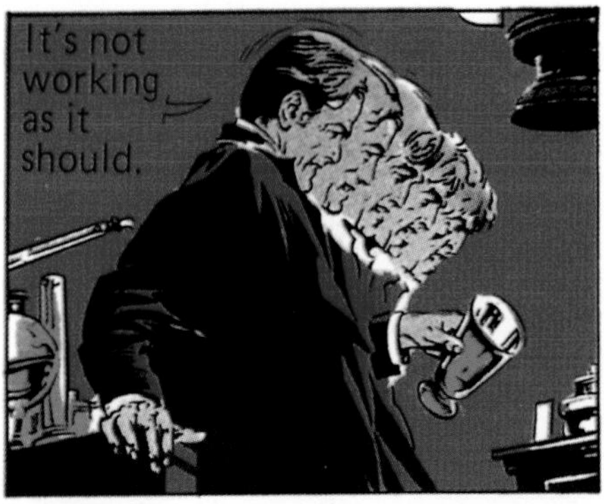
It's not working as it should.

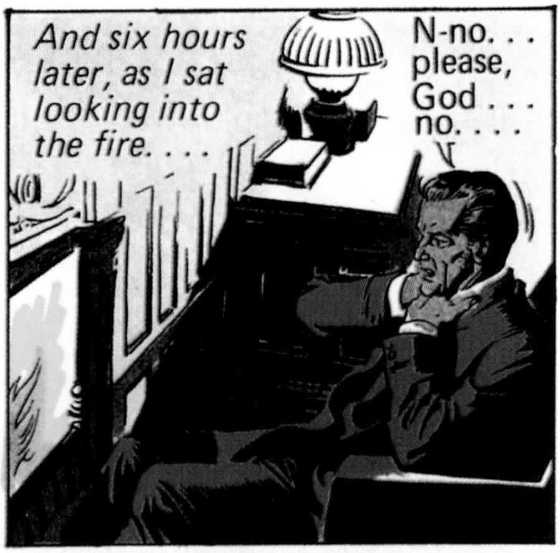
And six hours later, as I sat looking into the fire. . . .
N-no. . . please, God . . . no. . . .

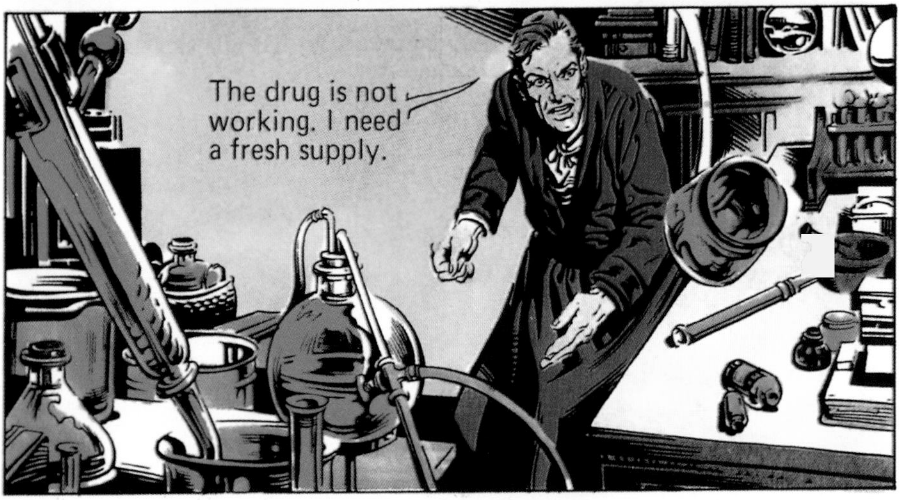
The drug is not working. I need a fresh supply.

A week later, Dr. Lanyon became ill, and in less than two weeks, he was dead.

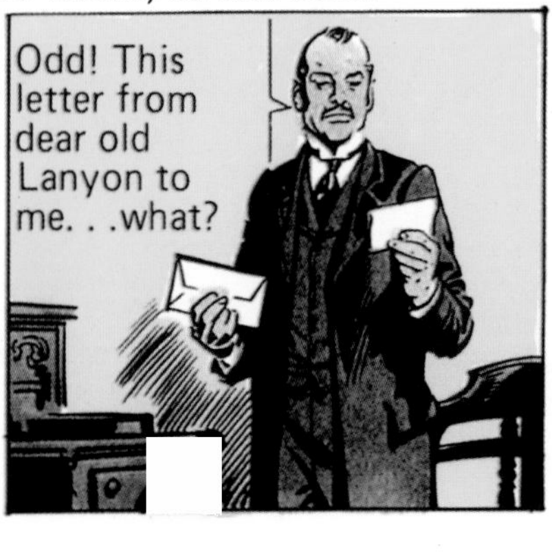
Odd! This letter from dear old Lanyon to me. . .what?

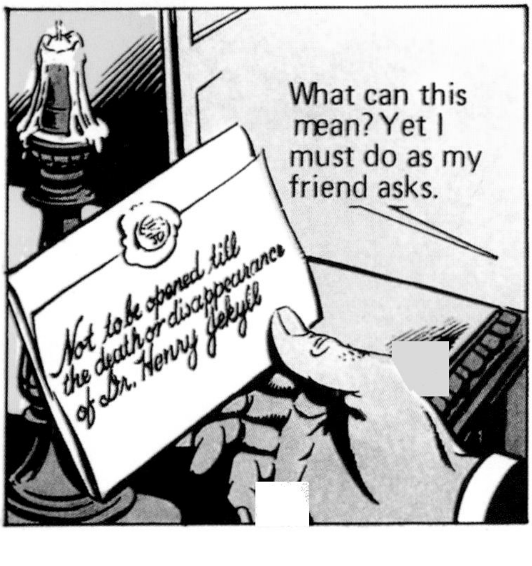
Not to be opened till the death or disappearance of Dr. Henry Jekyll
What can this mean? Yet I must do as my friend asks.

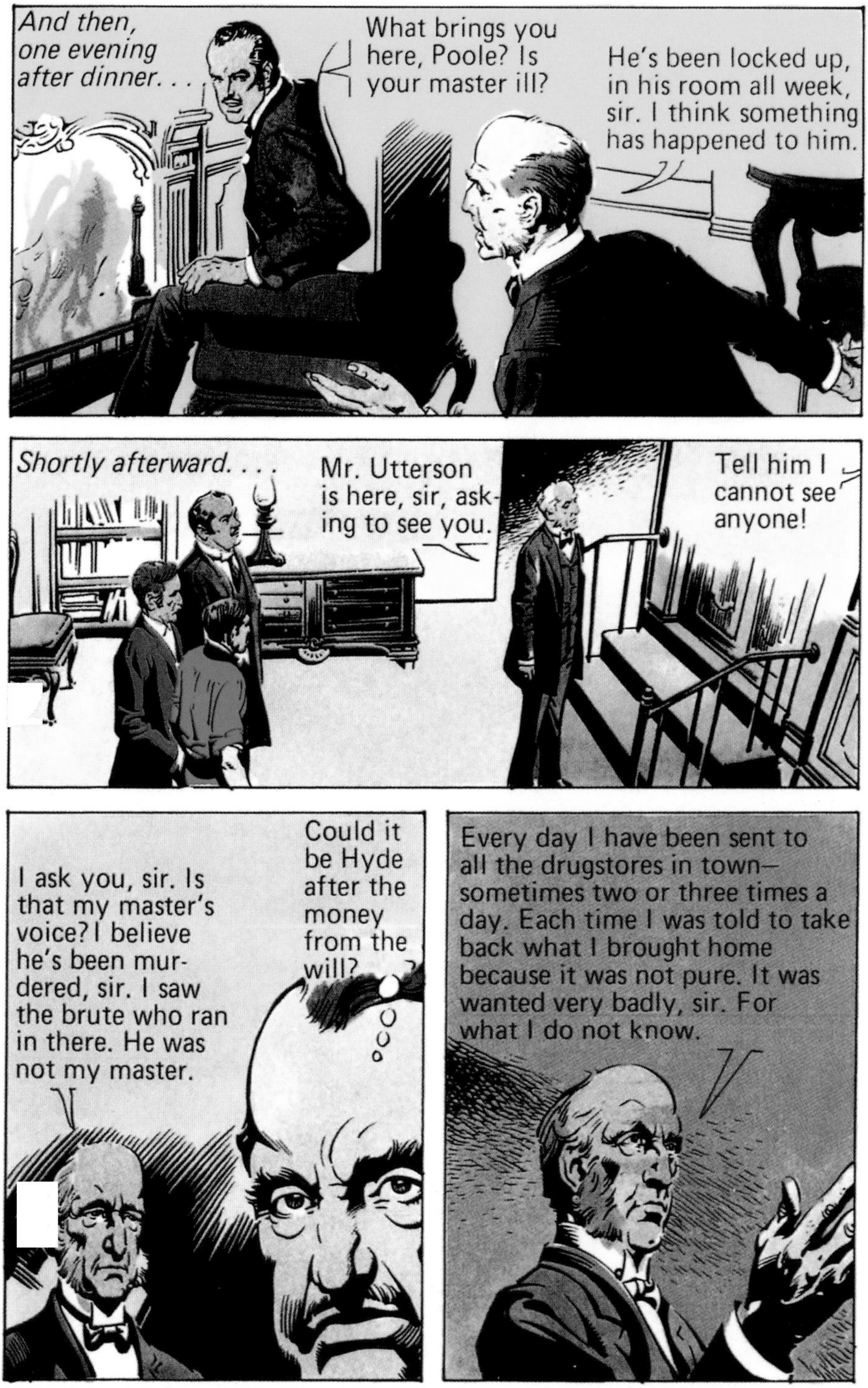
And then, one evening after dinner. . .
What brings you here, Poole? Is your master ill?
He's been locked up, in his room all week, sir. I think something has happened to him.
Shortly afterward. . . .
Mr. Utterson is here, sir, asking to see you.
Tell him I cannot see anyone!
I ask you, sir. Is that my master's voice? I believe he's been murdered, sir. I saw the brute who ran in there. He was not my master.
Could it be Hyde after the money from the will?
Every day I have been sent to all the drugstores in town—sometimes two or three times a day. Each time I was told to take back what I brought home because it was not pure. It was wanted very badly, sir. For what I do not know.

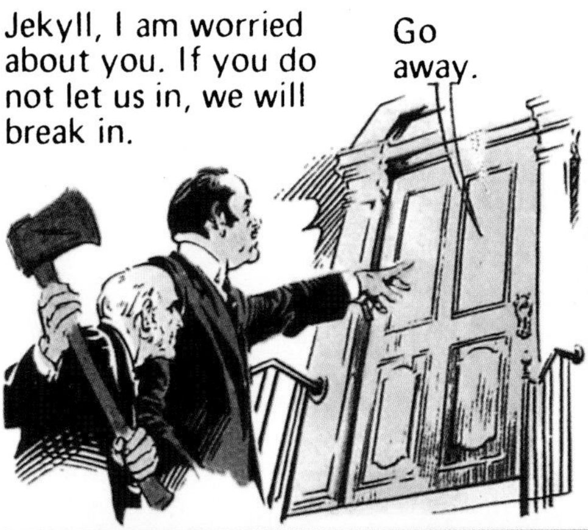
Jekyll, I am worried about you. If you do not let us in, we will break in.
Go away.

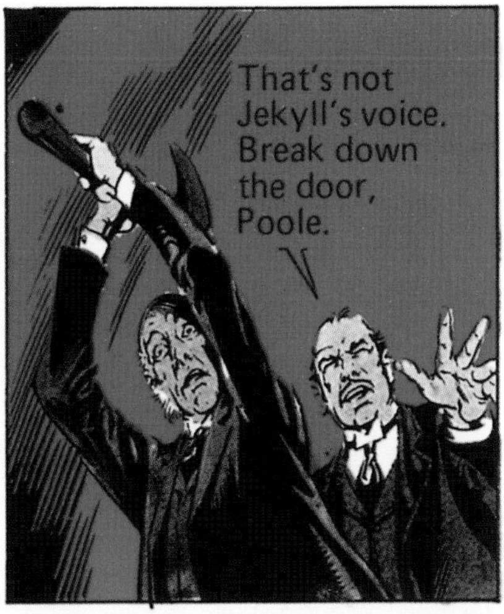
That's not Jekyll's voice. Break down the door, Poole.

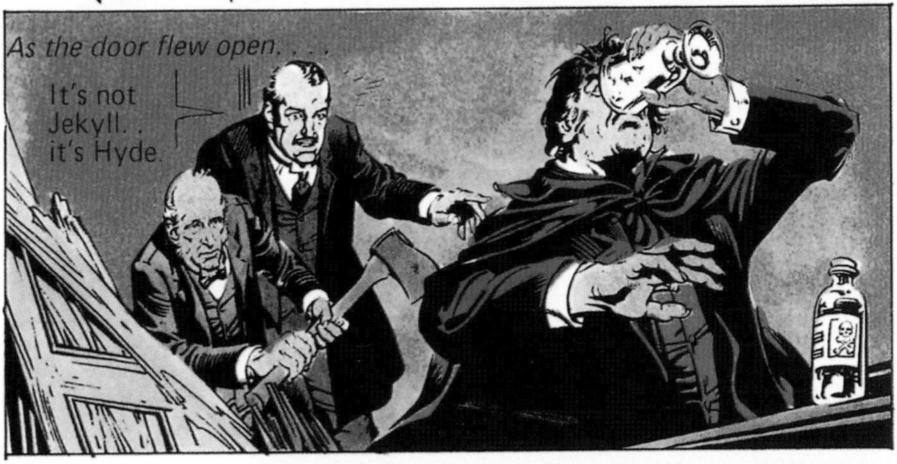
As the door flew open. . . .
It's not Jekyll. . it's Hyde.

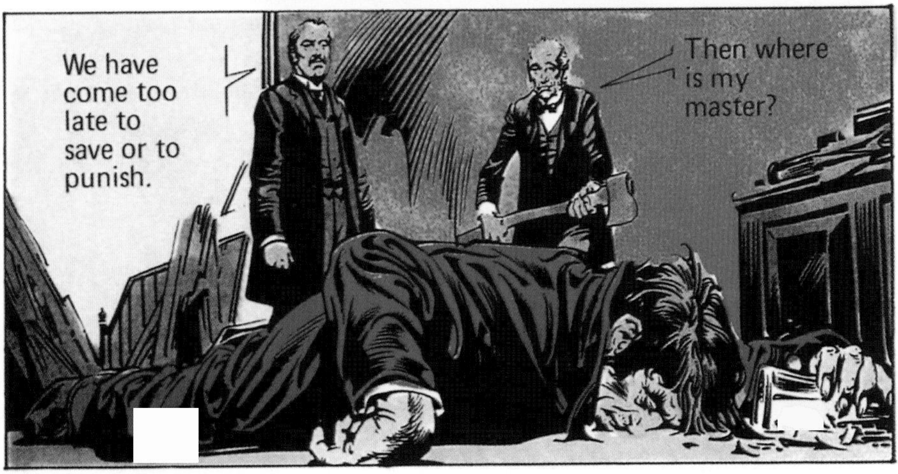
We have come too late to save or to punish.
Then where is my master?

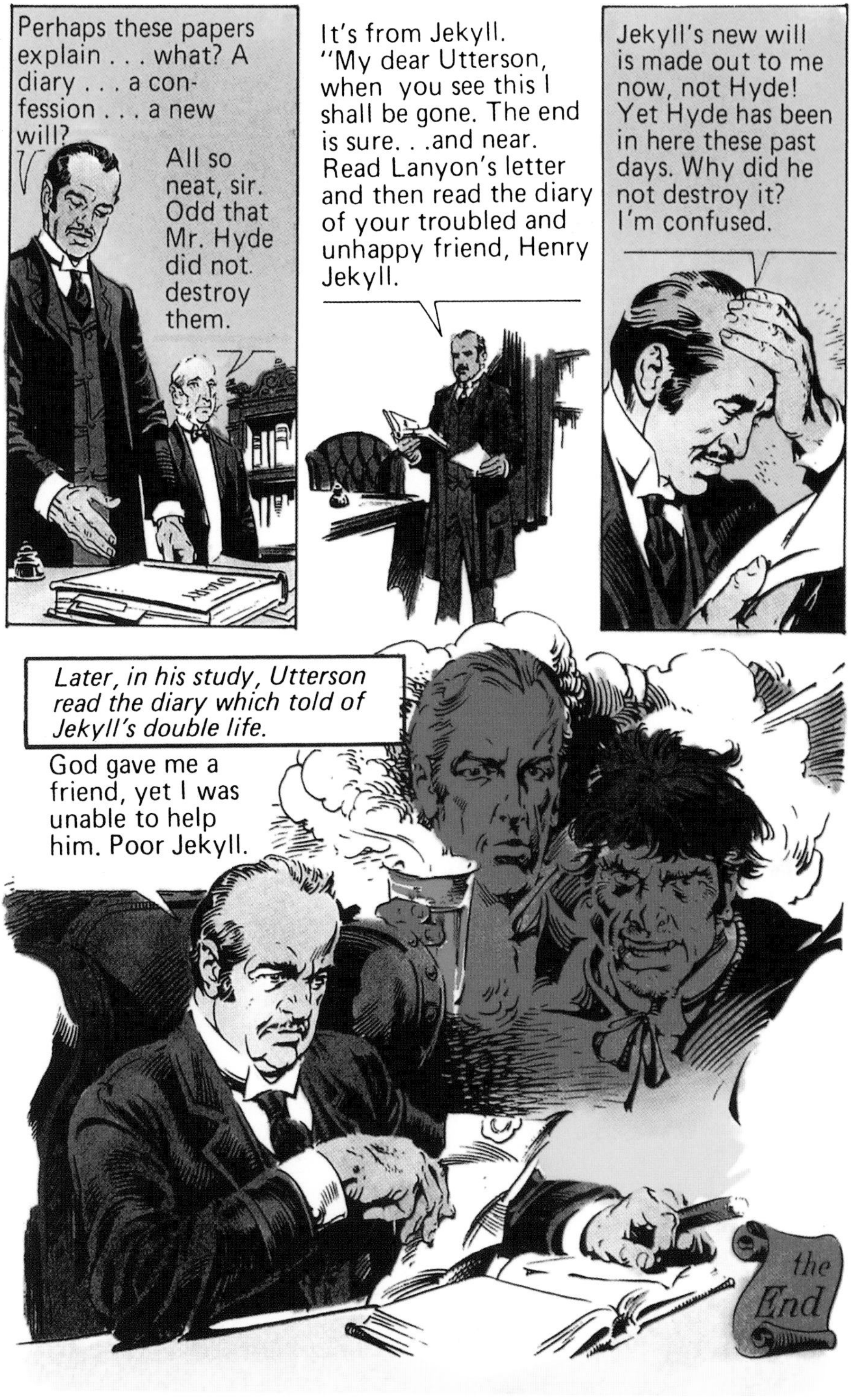
Perhaps these papers explain . . . what? A diary . . . a confession . . . a new will?
All so neat, sir. Odd that Mr. Hyde did not destroy them.
It's from Jekyll. "My dear Utterson, when you see this I shall be gone. The end is sure. . .and near. Read Lanyon's letter and then read the diary of your troubled and unhappy friend, Henry Jekyll.
Jekyll's new will is made out to me now, not Hyde! Yet Hyde has been in here these past days. Why did he not destroy it? I'm confused.
Later, in his study, Utterson read the diary which told of Jekyll's double life.
God gave me a friend, yet I was unable to help him. Poor Jekyll.
the End